HIGH-RISE MYSTERY

SHARNA JACKSON

KNIGHTS OF

Published by Knights Of
Knights Of Ltd, Registered Offices:
Kalculus, 119 Marylebone Road, London, NW1 5PU

www.knightsof.media
First published 2019
010

Written by Sharna Jackson
Text © Sharna Jackson, 2019
Cover art by Wumzum [Wumi Olaosebikan], 2019
Map illustration © Paul Coulbois (Astound US Inc.)
All rights reserved
The moral right of the author and illustrator has been asserted

Set in ITC Stone Serif / 12 pt
Design and Typeset by Marssaié Jordan
Printed and bound in the UK

A CIP catalogue record for this book will be available from the British Library

ISBN: PB: 978 1 99964 2518

10

Supported using public funding by
**ARTS COUNCIL
ENGLAND**

HIGH-RISE MYSTERY

lots of love!

x SJx

SHARNA JACKSON

To Joseph
Freddy I Yore

HIGH-RISE
MYSTERY

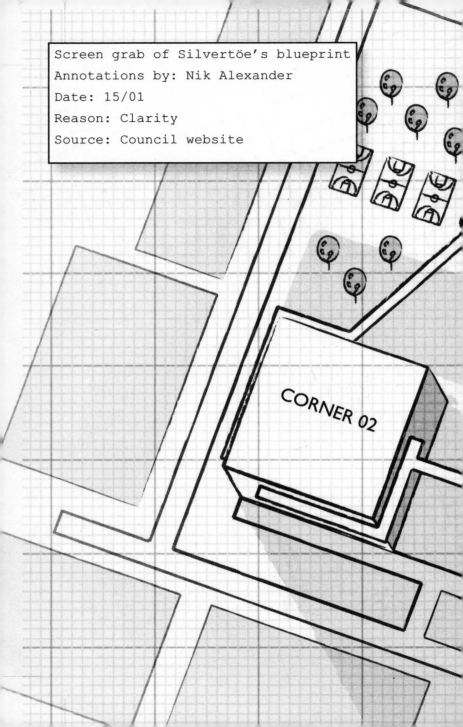

Screen grab of Silvertöe's blueprint
Annotations by: Nik Alexander
Date: 15/01
Reason: Clarity
Source: Council website

CORNER 02

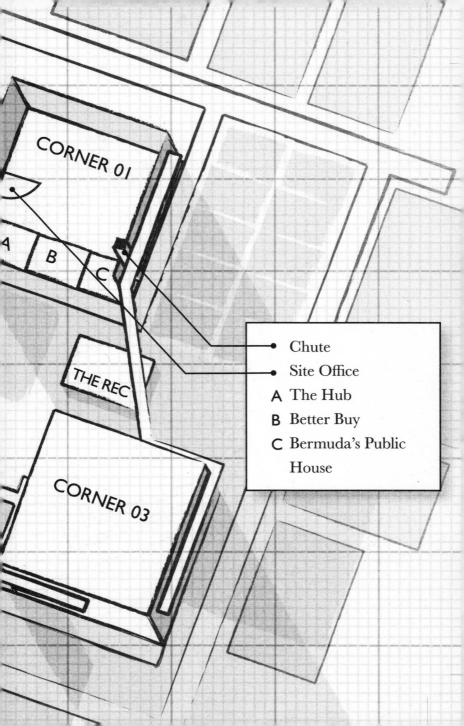

CORNER 01

A B C

THE REC

CORNER 03

• Chute
• Site Office
A The Hub
B Better Buy
C Bermuda's Public
  House

I

If you think finding a body is a fun adventure, you're 33% right.

Hugo Knightley-Webb, 45. Antiques dealer and occasional art teacher. Curly white hair. Straight-up dead.

This was a fact. One I could confirm personally because we − Norva and I − just found his body. 14:27 on July 23rd. The hottest day of the year so far. Thirty-five degrees, and rising.

We knew we'd find him. It wasn't coincidence or happenstance. No. We knew. But prior knowledge didn't make the discovery any less shocking or painful.

Or smelly.

We located the body using a system I call my Triangle of Truth. Naturally, it has three angles:

- Facts
- Evidence
- Deduction

That's just how I work. Me: Anika 'Nik' Alexander, 11. Science-led with a shaved head.

Norva Alexander, 13. My sister. Long braids, short temper. My partner in (solving) crime. She has her own system. She feels things in her:

- Stomach
- Bones
- Waters

Whatever waters are. I try not to think about Norva's liquids too much.

That's an apt summation of our collaboration, actually. Norva shouts theories and says seemingly stupid stuff. I then organise those words, and think about them critically. This is, according to Norva, teamwork. According to her, she's the Gut and I'm the Nut. I should be offended, but I'm not. I'm used to it.

To be fair to Norva, we both strongly suspected something was wrong through our noses. It smelled wrong on The Tri since Saturday. Dead wrong.

The Tri is, apparently, a very special estate. It doesn't feel like it to many of us, though. We made models of it in Art Club once. Straws and papier-mâché. Glue and gravel. Hugo said The Tri was a 'seminal example of Brutalism', but Hugo used to say a lot of random things.

He won't be saying so much now, unfortunately. Ugh, this situation is terrible. I promised myself I wouldn't cry. Again. I'll hold it together.

Yes, The Tri.

Norva says, 'These ends are a scorching hotbed for stories.'

She's not wrong. We've long-solved 'The Graffiti Games', 'Where the Ball At?' and 'The Cat Farm Chronicles'.

But this is different. Bigger. Scarier. Dangerous. The stakes are so much higher.

We'll start a real detective agency one day. A local business, for local people. Give something back to the estate. Our tagline would be: 'If something's going down at The Tri, we know what's up!'

Norva shouted 'Branding!' at the end of that sentence, and flicked her hair in my eyes.

So, that's why we – I – keep files. The Tri-Files. The files are a top-secret folder that includes but is not limited to:

- Logs
- Checklists
- Tables
- Photographs
- Screen grabs
- Recordings – both audio and video

Which we use to:

- Track movements
- Register events
- Keep logs
- Follow leads
- Find culprits
- Serve justice

I store the documents online so we can access and update them on our phones – and on our almost obsolete computer.

Where we go, they go. If we know, there are notes. The files – in this format and configuration – have been active for eleven months.

I won't ever stop updating them. Not now there is a real case, with a very real body. A body that belonged to someone I cared about.

Not now they're actually important. Not n[ow]
we need to find who did this to Hugo.

And why.

I gave Hugo fifteen minutes. If he didn't arrive at The Hub for Art Club by 14:15, our suspicions would be confirmed.

Dead. Dead since Saturday morning.

Hugo was notoriously punctual, and had only been late for Art Club once – last Christmas.

It was only two minutes, but he burst into The Hub at 14:02; super red-faced, full white beard, sweating in the snow. A tardy, arty Santa. He was incredibly apologetic and disappointed in himself. I swear he swore under his breath. Hugo told us [well, just me – everyone else was late, too] that 'being late was disrespectful of everyone's time – the most precious resource of all'.

Hard agree. Lateness is rudeness.

Now, I was on edge. My nerves? Utterly frayed.

Please don't be late Hugo. Please. Not today.
Welcome to the tensest fifteen minutes of my life.

***

Norva and I arrived at The Hub at 13:50. Art Club was
due to begin at 14:00.

'What we doing today, again?' asked Norva.
'The poster's not on the door.'

I reached for my phone, and scrolled to a picture
I took of it last week.

I held my breath.

'Today's topic is "Ancient Egyptian Death
Masks", Norva,' I said slowly.

I hoped it was ironic.

I hoped it were something we could all laugh
hysterically about later, at home, over tall glasses of juice
and green salads.

Norva chuckled. 'If that's not an omen, I don't
know what is!'

It wasn't funny to me, at all. I rolled my eyes at
her, while my heart fluttered in my chest.

Ancient Egyptian Death Masks. Really, Hugo?

I preferred the sciences, definitely − but art
classes with Hugo tended to be:

- Fun
- Interesting
- Confusing

I understand about 60%, to be generous. What Hugo says about art doesn't make sense to me. How is a messy, unfresh bed art? Or rows of bricks? It's utterly perplexing.

I liked how he talked and cared about it, though. I loved it.

At 13:51, Norva pushed open the double doors into the Hub.

'Oh my days,' she gasped. 'It's like opening the oven when your roast is ready. Blast furnace levels in here.'

She fanned her face dramatically and slumped against the wall.

The Hub is a large, frankly grubby room where Tri residents:

- Hold meetings
- Classes
- Celebrate births, deaths and marriages

It has a number of distinguishing marks. The top three are:

• Scuffmarks

Kids have skidded and slid across this floor in black-soled shoes for decades.

• A large, sooty burn on the south wall

Date of first appearance: 18/08.

Last summer, someone [chief suspect: Barry West. 62. Grey hair. Purple face. Yellow teeth. Landlord of on-site bar Bermuda's next door] decided to have an ill-advised impromptu indoor barbeque, which, evidently, got out of hand.

The Tri-Files began that very day.

I felt bad for our dad, aka Pap. 39. Aka Joseph Alexander. Single dad, sadly. Dances so, so badly.

As the Head Caretaker at The Tri, he has attempted to cover [in Tri Yellow – the estate's default paint] that burn three times, but it returns without fail.

Norva says, the burn is 'iconic' and claims it reminds her of 'Jesus at Easter, on a constant comeback'.

•Hugo's teaching desk with matching chair

Both are fashioned from dark mahogany wood and cracked forest green leather. They look – and smell – old and expensive.

I 'helped' Hugo and Pap move it here when I was eight. Hugo really appreciated my 'directions' and smiled at my 'guidance'.

I smiled at the memory. I liked helping Hugo. He usually set out tables, chairs and art materials around his desk, in the morning before class. If I was early – and I normally was – I'd help too.

Today, the tables and chairs were stacked against the east side of the room, next to the chair cupboard.

There was no sign of the materials.

At 13:52, we noticed a poster [hand-drawn, black biro, poorly photocopied] on the west wall for last Friday's Tri-Angel meeting – the estate's fundraising and volunteer group.

I knew the artist. Chief Tri-Angel and manager of The Hub. 'Charity' Jane Cooper. 42. Overly sweet. Never sour.

I shook my head. We should have been at that meeting, without a doubt.

But no, we were at home instead. Watching *Death in Paradise* [aka DiP].

It's Norva's favourite – a murder mystery show on the BBC. She waited – an impatient – eight months and twelve days for the new series. It's too good to watch on iPlayer, apparently.

'DiP on Catch up?' she spat, last Friday evening. 'How very dare you?' she said, looking me up and down with her eyes.

So that was that. She had to see it in real time, and I had to be there to capture her reactions.

Missing that meeting had – potentially – set us back.

There were gaps in our knowledge.
Gaps we'd need to fill – urgently – if we were right about Hugo.

We opened the windows at 13:53. We put five tables and ten chairs out around Hugo's desk. My head and my upper lip were dripping sweat, but who wouldn't sweat in this heat?

Pap, I supposed.

He's in decent shape.

I thought about our neighbours. Who else was healthy?

Mrs Kowalski, definitely. She's surprisingly fit.

Flat 222. Next door to us. Looks between sixty and a hundred and fifty, depending on the light. 5'0".

So strong, for an old lady. Constantly carrying carrier bags.

I laughed at a mental image of her.
She was dressed as a Victorian strongman. A hundred Tesco bags at each end of a barbell.

I was distracting myself with silly thoughts.
'Focus, Nik! Concentrate!' I said to myself.
'What?' asked Norva.
'Nothing.'
We sat. We waited.

3

Footsteps at 13:56! The door opened. We jumped in our seats. I looked over to Norva; her eyes were wide and wet.

But it wasn't Hugo. My heart sank.

It was George Shah. 13. Tall. Thin. Music is life.

He sauntered into the room. 'Yes yes, NSquared How do?'

NSquared is our 'couple name', according to George. I hated to admit that I kind of liked it. Mathematical and logical.

I nodded at George, while Norva high-fived him. He looked around The Hub.

'Yo, it's super sparse in here today,' he said, his hand to his chin. 'Where Hugo at? Ole boy is normally raring to go at this point, no?'

He would be, normally. He should be! 'Yes,' I said. 'No sign of him all weekend, actually. It's slightly concerning.' Lies. It was so much more than 'slightly' concerning.

'Oh seen?' said a surprised George. He narrowed his eyes. 'You got a case brewing? It might have legs you know…'

Norva's interest was immediately piqued. 'How so?'

George crouched next to Norva. 'Hugo didn't look too fresh at Friday's meeting. Not good at all. He was struggling with the heat, big time. Then – that stuff with him and your dad. That was nuts…' He shook his head.

Stuff with our dad?

'What stuff with Pap?' I asked loudly.

Norva spun her head around to look at me with confused and concerned eyes.

Ring! Ring!

George's phone.

He put his hand up to us, to pause our conversation while he answered his call.

'Yes, yes, Mum. Alright? Alright. Alright! I'm on it, OK? Cool your jets. I'm coming.'

It was Nina. Nina Shah, 37. Short, small body. Long, dark hair. George ended his call.

'Listen both, I gotta bounce, I...'

Norva wasn't having it. 'George!' She shouted. 'What the hell! It's Monday afternoon. The meeting was Friday night!' She kissed her teeth, but she wasn't finished. 'We just getting into this now?' She ranted. 'What's your deal? What timeline are we living on? Clearly one where you don't keep me in the loop!'

George smiled. He, like me, was used to this Norva.

'Ayyy, Norv, behave. Listen, first of all, I wasn't even supposed to be there. My mum literally dragged me. Saying she wanted to join them Tri-Angels. Not now, though. Allow that! Anyway, be glad I went, because it was flames and fire. Big. Secondly, I did text you, innit. But you think you're all that. Leaving me on read. I see you.'

Norva looked down. 'Oh yeah, I was deep in DiP.'

George slapped her on the back. 'Yeah, I bet you were. I'll fill you in later, swear down, but I gotta check in with Mum. Family first, you know how it goes. In a bit.'

George pushed the double doors and left.

4

There was still no sign of Hugo at 14:03.

He had now – officially – broken his record for lateness.

I waved my phone at Norva, shaking my head. 'It's three minutes past two.'

'Yeah, I know,' she said, shaking her wrists. 'Something is definitely up. This feeling in my bones is amping up. They're starting to tingle, you know?'

No, I didn't know.
But I hoped all 206 bones in her body would rattle some sense into her.

How could we have missed that meeting?

I clenched my fist. Anger distracted me.
I hated my sister. No, I didn't. That was a bit strong.

I certainly hated her obsession with that *Death in Paradise* show, though.

It's not even good.

'Nik!' I whispered to myself. 'Focus.'

I unclenched my fist and my palms were wet with sweat. I struggled to hold my phone.

I looked closely at my hands. They're about a third of the size of Hugo's.

That's an exaggeration, mostly, but his hands were huge.

We all traced our hands for a display we made for Diwali at Art Club once. We had to take his out – it completely disrupted the pattern. Hugo himself said he 'unbalanced the work'. His disappointment was palpable.

He removed his hands from the work, and drummed his fingers against his lips, with wet eyes. Thinking about wetness reminded me just how dry my mouth was.

I needed a Vitonica, desperately.

Serena makes Vitonica – that's Serena Knightley-Webb. 38. Blonde, thin, tall, entrepreneur. Hugo's sister.

Vitonica is named after two of Serena's favourite things: her mother, Veronica (RIP) and vitamins. When I tried my first one, Serena told me that 'the juices cleanse and balance one's system'.

I didn't know about that, but I did know that they're delicious and sweet and satisfying and calming and I love them and I need them. I needed one right now.

My name's Nik, and I have a juice problem.

I thought about Serena. She's been a resident on The Tri for eighteen weeks and one day, now. When she moved in, she told us that her and her husband had 'consciously-uncoupled'.

That meant they broke up, in Plain English. They used to live in a large house in West London, but he kept that even though she paid for half of it. How that's fair, I didn't know. Now she's in a flat, with her brother, in South East London.

A hard-core downgrade for some, but not Serena.

She loved The Tri, and The Tri loved her back. Me included.

If you needed her, she'd be there. She'd worked hard to fit in.

She ran:

- a yoga group
- a dog sitting and walking service
- a Facebook group for the residents

Vitonica was her newest venture. Juices made from fruits from The Garden, and then sold in Better Buy. She wanted a stall at Whitford Market, next to Hugo's pitch. The plan was to sell the juices for double The Tri price and donate all the proceeds back to the estate. Inspirational.

I looked at my phone.

14:05. Still no Hugo.

'Let's review the Receipts,' Norva sighed. 'Let me back these bad feelings and bone-tingles up with some facts. Time's a tick-tocking.'

'The Receipts' is what Norva called `The Tri-Files` sometimes. I don't understand why. They had a perfectly acceptable name already.

She reached for her phone. I pushed my chair closer to hers to see her screen.

Our sweaty forearms velcroed together immediately. My stomach flipped. It was going for gold in Olympic diving.

'Open `Tri_Thoughts.doc` and scroll backwards, please?' I asked.

Norva read – and acted – out her words. Of course she did.

```
Saturday morning, 10:30 roughly.

Hotter than hell.

The lift has been out on Corner One for TWO DAYS
so I walked Ringo on Third Avenue, outside the
```

flats on floor 21, for his morning wee. Something is RIPE in the trash chute. Bare unfresh. Next level.

The bin bros are still striking. 138 hours and counting according to Nik. Council need to pay up, STAT.

BUT BUT BUT!

I'm not convinced this is just trash, doing its trash thing, living its trash life. My waters say no. It's different. I went to check it out, so embarked on the epic odyssey that is Going Down The Stairs. Me and Ringo like LITERALLY sniffed about a bit, then crossed The Rec for some fresher(?) air. Asked a few people about the stench. No one thinks it's shady!? Not one! This lot are no-nose having zombies, I swear. Pap reckons it could be the sequel to The Summer of Infinite Nappies (Never Forget) but I remember those. Not having it. NOT the same. Nope.

It's well hard to describe the smell in words and not through contemporary dance – but here goes. It's just so off, like sweet and sour and musty and flowery and also, importantly, like many shades of poop all at the same time. Like, I just don't like it.

5

14:08. Hugo's still late. I silently smirked at my rhyme, then shook my smile away.

I had to focus. Again.

'So, the stench began on Saturday. Confirmed,' I said with a sigh, back in the moment.

'Seen,' said Norva. 'And it smells even worse today, right – like getting worse every minute? What else we got for Saturday?'

'Open `Bedroom_Window_Logs.doc`, **Norva**. There will be more info in there.'

The document took its sweet time to load. Norva drummed her fingers on the desk impatiently. These entries started ten months and two weeks ago – when Pap got me the telescope for my eleventh birthday. Norva had written a note with it that said: 'We might be in the gutter, but we're definitely looking at the stars'.

She's looked at the stars with it precisely never. She quickly found other uses for it, closer to earth, though.

The Telescope Tales — her title, my words:

Hugo leaves for Whitford Market by 06:30 on Saturday morning, without fail. Today his van remained on The Tri. This was a fact. We checked at 09:55, 15:00, 17:00 and 21:00.

The van has a permanent parking spot (to the chagrin of other car owners on the estate) at the entrance to Better Buy, 'blocking' the view. We know that Mark normally appears at approximately 10:00 to get:

• milk (full-fat, four pints)
• a magazine about 'celebrities' for his mother
• cream for his spots

Today, we couldn't see him. Norva was disappointed and looked dejected until 10:13, when she left to walk Ringo.

That's Mark Walker. 16. Young. Dull. Broke. Norva is convinced they're 'endgame' – whatever that means – and will live together on The Tri within the next ten years.

To Norva, Mark is mysterious and strong. To me, he's basic and she's easily impressed.

He works with Pap evenings, weekends and during the holidays. He needs the money. He's more of a hindrance than help, according to Pap, but Norva thinks Pap is 'hashtag blessed' to spend honest time with him.

Norva was also thirsty at 14:11.

I was too – but I was mostly scared.

Hugo, come on. Please.

I made a quick list of other things I liked about Hugo:

• the glasses he wore on a chain

• the way he peered over them when he was making a point

• his rings – one on each finger. Gaudy but great

At 14:13 Norva stared straight ahead at Barry's Burn. She smiled, slightly, but I didn't know why.

0% of this situation was amusing to me.

None of it.

She glanced at her phone.

'Two minutes until the deadline,' she said, with a horrid chuckle.

At the stroke of 14:14, I reached for Norva's hand. She swatted it away.

'Don't be ridiculous,' she muttered.

14:15.

My heart sank.

'Time's up' Norva said. 'Let's go.'

6

Norva pushed the table away from us with both hands, stood to attention and announced loudly – to no one – 'Alexanders OUT, bozos!'

Summoning me to join her with her eyes, Norva tossed her braids over her shoulder and turned on her heel. She stomped out of The Hub, busting through the double doors, letting them swing back into my face.

Welcome to my life.

I followed her into the searing heat on The Tri. I despise the sun. Hate it. It's undoubtedly my least favourite celestial body. Summer is my personal sweaty hell.

I winced at the heat and light. I put my back against the wall, in a quick, practical attempt to stay in the shade. The wall was roasting hot too. I leapt away.

'Why you out here cringing like Dracula accidently catching dawn's first rays, Nik? Get it together,' Norva said. She threw out her arm and pointed, her head back. 'To the bins!'

Was this a game to her?

We passed Better Buy and waved hello to Sissy St. Claire, 59. Wheelchair. Church on Sunday. Gossip all week.

Sissy offered us a wilted wave in return from behind her till.

Hugo's van was parked outside the shop. I noticed it immediately, naturally, but Norva slapped me on the back, and used two fingers to point at the van and her eyes repeatedly to ensure I saw it.

'Clock it,' she said in a low voice.

I nodded in dehydrated agreement. 'I see it.' I peered inside the van's rear windows. There were piles of open, awkwardly stacked boxes. I took a photo, pinched and zoomed into it to take a closer look.

Junk to me. Antiques to Hugo.

Norva shouted to Sissy from the doorway, her hands on her hips. 'You seen Hugo, Sis?'

Sissy shook her head. 'No, girls, not since the meeting.'

'What time?' I asked, stepping away from the van.

I pulled out my phone and opened `Tri_Thoughts.doc`.

'Welllll, I was one of the last to leave, was chatting with Mrs Kowalski. You know it's been four years since Our Lord took her husband?'

Sissy made the sign of the cross over her chest and looked to the sky. 'God bless his soul! Four years on Friday! Time is the master, but...'

'The time, Sissy? What time?' I broke in. I had to. Life's too short for her sermons.

'Welllll, I got home just after eleven, so he was gone by ten thirty. Yes. Definitely.'

Sissy inched closer to her fan. 'He left with Serena, after your dad stormed out. Jane came back to lock up just before eleven and kicked us out. Then I went home and watched *Death in Paradise* on catch up.'

I spoke to Sissy, but stared at Norva. '*Death in Paradise*? On catch up? How convenient.'

Norva fixed her eyes to the floor.

'I know!' replied Sissy. 'Living in the future is truly a blessing.'

'It really is,' I said.

'Thanks Sissy,' Norva muttered through tight lips as we left the shop.

We ducked beneath the broken window of Bermuda's (chief suspect: Barry). Norva touched the 'Don't Get Lost In This Triangle' graffiti, spray-painted on the glazed bricks below (chief suspect: Barry).

Inside the pub, a glass smashed. The residents shouted 'aaaaaaaayyyyyyyy' in unison and clapped in appreciation. Norva thrust her head through the shattered window, millimetres away from a definite decapitation.

'Yo Barry? Is Hugo in there?' she shouted.

Barry stood behind the bar, laughing at the spilt drink. 'No – haven't seen him all weekend. Wasn't at the lock-in after the meeting on Friday night, or on Saturday night. Thought he'd be here on Sunday, but he's not answering his phone. If you see him, tell him he's a mug! Joking, joking, we love him really.'

The pub's patrons broke into song. 'We love you Hugo, we do!'

'What's a 'lock-in'?' I asked, pushing Norva out of the way, ready to expand my notes.

'Doesn't matter,' shouted Barry over the singing. 'Forget I said that. Don't remember to tell your dad either.'

Barry and the whole pub laughed.

We nodded our thanks and moved on. Ten metres from the bins, the smell became sharper.

Stronger with each step.

Loud music played in a flat high above us.

The bass thumped in my chest and down to my toes.

My heart beat fast, in time with the song.

I inched forward, but Norva pulled me back.

'Now, Nik,' she said, holding on to my arm, 'prepare yourself. If Hugo's really in there, you know he's going to look rough, right? Real bad. Like a zombie, probably.'

She laughed, putting her arms stiffly in front of her, crossing her eyes. 'He might want braaaainssss. Luckily, your baldhead gives him easy access. Om nom nom.'

Confirmation received. This was still a game.

'You're not funny, Norva,' I said. 'Not at all.'

My bottom lip trembled. My eyes grew moist.

Norva threw her hands in the air. 'I'm sure it's just a fox in there, Nik.'

Her hand on my shoulder, her smile dimmed. 'That's what I'm telling myself, anyway.'

7

We pushed open the doors to the refuse area and were instantly welcomed by the resident colony of flies.

'Whoa ...' Norva whispered out of the corner of her mouth.

My eyes watered immediately. I blinked quickly, five, times to clear them.

There were a considerable number of bin bags. I estimated sixty-eight. Approximately a third had split open and 95% of those were melting, fermenting or a combination of both.

I noted:

- cans: bean, beer, beef (corned)
- papers: news, walls, sand
- fruit: off, rotting, rotted

Norva elbowed me, pointing out a bottle of Vitonica. Well, Vitonica in a previous life. In its current form, it was a globulous, congealing, fruity lava lamp of doom.

Norva rubbed her stomach sarcastically and licked her lips.

I opened my mouth to offer a witty retort. Regrets. A large fly flew into my mouth. I spat it out and rubbed at my face. Norva laughed through tight lips.

I held my breath as much as I could as my eyes streamed. I wasn't sure where to start. I looked at Norva for guidance.

Norva jabbed her finger at the large metal skip directly under the chute.

'Whatever's dead is buried in there. Get in,' she said, between her fingers. 'You're bald, wear the same outfit every day AND take up less space.'

I shook my head vigorously.

'ALSO, I've got two years on you, so deal with it. You have no choice.'

0% chance.

I'll admit it. In some – minimal – ways, I look up to Norva. But lines and limits exist.

'I can't do this,' I replied. I rubbed my arm. 'I can't.' I shook my head. 'No.'

It didn't take much to convince her.

Norva shrugged. 'Alright, fine, whatever. I'm going in.'

She twisted her braids into a topknot, and tied them with a black band she always kept around her wrist.

If I was right about Hugo, I was sure she would want the glory. Whatever the glory of finding a corpse in a skip is.

8

Norva threw her cross-body bag at me and rummaged through the pockets of her floral summer dress, checking they were empty.

A single tissue fell to the floor, which she ignored. Littering is offensive, but since the whole room was literally a bin, she got a pass. This time.

Norva leaned over and tightened the ankle straps on her sandals. She walked five steps towards the skip, getting a measure of it and paced backwards five steps and performed two squats.

She stood up, put her hands on her hips and rolled them side to side, three times.
She then rolled her head to the left, and then to the right.
She stretched her arms straight forwards and cracked her knuckles.

She sighed.

Increasingly exasperated at her inappropriately-timed exercise routine, I began: 'Norva are you going t…'

'Now!' she shouted. She ran at the skip and jumped, cat-like onto it. She gripped its edges, pulling herself up and into it.

It was impressive. The workout was worth it.

Once inside, Norva looked down at me from the top, her lips tucked under her teeth, her eyes wide. She shrugged, took a very misguided deep breath and violently coughed.

It was time.

Putrid rubbish bags flew out of the skip.

Norva's head popped up. 'Oh my days,' she said quietly. 'Nik…'

'What…?' I asked cautiously, not knowing if I actually wanted to know.

'Look at this.'

As I jumped at the skip, I thought of Ringo. 7, but 42 in human years, roughly. Our black, white and tan Jack Russell.

He does that jump when he wants something you're eating.

Inside the skip, Norva struggled to lift a large paint can.

The can was grey with a peeling white label that claimed it held 20lts – a significant amount of paint.

I assumed it was still full, because it was clearly so heavy. Either that, or Norva was being particularly weak.

Judging by the familiar colour of congealed off-white paint around the lid, it was the official paint used everywhere on The Tri.

'OK...it's a can of Tri paint...'

'Come on, no, look,' she said, 'at the bottom.' She pointed.

I moved down the skip. I jumped up again and again. Ringo – if he had feelings for anyone other than himself – would have been proud.

At the bottom was a sticky dark brown stain. Stuck to the stain were a few curly white hairs. Familiar, curly white hairs.

Oh no.

I stopped jumping and stood up straight. Stiff as a board. Norva took a shocked step back into the skip and nearly lost her footing.

'Norva,' I started slowly. 'This is getting real. Too real. Get out. Now. We need Pap.'

'I know, but we're so close though?'

'So close to what, Norva?' I shouted at her. 'Being scarred for life!?'

'No,' she replied flatly. 'The truth.'

She dived back into the skip, threw a bag by my feet. It burst on my trainer.

'Oh no, Nik...' she started.

'No. Don't. Don't say it, please.'

'I've found him.'

My stomach twisted. My intestines rearranged themselves into knots. Pretzels.

'Nik,' Norva pleaded, breaking my thoughts. 'Come clock this. Tell me I'm wrong.'

Norva threw her arm down for me.

I closed my eyes and grabbed it. She pulled me up and I opened my eyes, blinking twice to focus.

There were positives.

And negatives.

Positives: no blood, guts or gore.

Negatives: a clearly body-shaped, heavy-duty human-sized bin bag.

I recognized the bag, instantly. It was one of the special bags we've seen Pap and Mark use when working on flats here.

Strong and robust.

Perfect for moving a body.

'Norva, this is a bag. We can't be sure that...'
I began, lying to myself.

Norva nudged the bag with her foot and an arm
flopped out of the top. On the hand was a ring on each
finger. This was a body and this body was Hugo.

The game was over.

9

A wail grew from deep inside me. I opened my mouth and it left my body, loudly. Hot tears streamed down my face, as we ran, hand in hand, full pelt across The Tri.

At top speed, I glimpsed Sissy in Better Buy. She looked up, briefly. She rolled her eyes and put her face dangerously close to the blades of her fan.

We ran to the lobby of Corner One and entered, panting, walk-running, rushing to Pap's office in the control room.

He needed to know. Immediately.

We burst through his door and Pap was on the telephone, laughing. I'd never heard him laugh like that before.

'It's done. It's done. Everything is in place. Can't wait to see you later,' he said in a low voice. He was smiling to whomever he was speaking to.

I didn't recognise this Pap. He sounded like Norva did, when she talked about Mark. He sounded... romantic? It was both uncomfortable and disgusting.

'Pap! Pap!' Norva shouted. 'Oh my god, Dad!'

Norva burst into tears. Pap looked panicked, his eyes widened. He dropped his phone onto his desk.

'What girls?' he said, standing up shakily, seeming both embarrassed and concerned. 'What's happened? Are you alright?'

'No, Pap. We're not,' I replied. 'Hugo's in the bin.'

Pap looked confused. I could see him rapidly evaluating and discarding the potential meanings of this sentence.

'He's dead,' I clarified.

Pap's eyes widened, his hand flew to his mouth. 'Oh NO. NO!' he shouted, snatching his phone and stuffing it into his pocket.

He winced as he performed a painful-looking hobble-run hybrid to the door, stumbling past us.

We followed as he attempted to run across The Tri, shuffling with each step. This was new.

To me at least.

Norva and I grabbed his hands and rushed him to the refuse room.

His eyes widened at the smell. He gagged.

Pap didn't need animal-like prowess to see into the skip, being so tall. He stepped forward and peered in.

'Hugo,' he whispered under his breath, as he shook his head slowly. Pap pulled out his mobile and jabbed in three numbers.

'Hello, Police?' He used his polite phone voice. 'This is Joseph Alexander, Estate Manager at The Triangle. Yes. There's a body in the refuse area of Corner One; it looks like resident Hugo Knightley-Webb.' He limp-walked in quick circles as he talked.

'Girls,' he said, covering up the phone's mouthpiece. 'Go outside, get some fresh air.'

Norva and I pushed open the doors and sat cross-legged, backs against the wall. My body ached and my mind raced. I looked over at Norva, who stared straight ahead, silently.

'The Police are on their way,' Pap said.

He collected us from the floor and drew us into a hug.

'Stupid thing to ask, but are you OK?' he said.

I nodded, knowing it was a stupid gesture to make. We were 2.5% OK.

'That was a terrible, terrible thing to see,' he continued. 'Talk to me about it and, if you want, I'll sort someone for you to see. To talk to. Maybe you'll see Katie today? Hopefully.'

That was comforting.

We missed Katie Smyth, 25. Black hair, blue eyes, brilliant.

Katie used to live here, until recently, three months ago. She was a Corner One-dweller, like us. She lived in Flat 193. She looked after us, and we looked up to her. Since we were five and seven.

This is sort of Katie's fault. I blame her. Norva's love of stories – mysteries in particular – leads back to Katie.

We spent 65% of evenings and weekends watching Katie watching one of the following:

- The Bill
- Midsomer Murders
- The Inspector Lynley Mysteries

Once she finished her Certificate in Knowledge of Policing [which we helped her study for], and passed her probation [thanks to us], she moved out of The Tri. Pastures new.

We missed her, but she was only two estates and three streets away.

Pap cuddled us tightly. Too tightly actually; it was hard to breathe.

'I'm so sorry,' he said. 'I'm so, so sorry. Especially for you, Nik, I know how much you liked him.'

I shrugged silently, betraying just how much I liked Hugo.

Liked Hugo. Past tense.

'Girls,' Pap said, finally breaking the circle and sniffing. 'I say this with love, but you smell. Badly. Go home, wash yourselves and check on Ringo? The lift is fixed now, so don't walk up.'

10

Norva pushed button 22. The doors closed, and we were slowly, creakily, pulled to the top floor of Corner One.

The bulb inside the lift had been blown for seven weeks, two days. A non-urgent fix. Natural light came through in blinding bursts as we passed each floor.

It was oppressively hot. One positive, though. No one else was waiting to use the lift. A straight run all the way up: one of the simplest – yet most satisfying – pleasures of living on The Tri.

I blinked away the fresh tears that were starting to form.

'Yep, Pap's right. Ringo, then wash,' said Norva. Beams of light ran rhythmically across her face. 'But, also, obviously, more importantly, it's time to start putting this case together, right?'

Her eyes shone in the dark.

'It's really time,' she whispered.

She was right. It was. I nodded.

This is what we do. It had never been more important. Or so painful. I wiped my eyes and began to pack my feelings into a box. To be unlocked another time. Later.

The time to focus was now.

'Facts. Evidence. Deduction.' I said, exhaling. 'I'll start a file.'

I reached for my phone and opened a new document. We arrived on our floor with a shudder and the doors creaked open.

Someone was leaning against the wall opposite the lift. I squinted.

Mrs Kowalski. She had five heavy plastic shopping bags bound around the wrist of her left arm. They left ruby red tracks on her thin white skin.

Mrs Kowalski breathed heavily, sweat drip dropped from her face onto the floor. Her excessively large, round glasses slipped down her nose. She was 'serving that owl realness' as Norva had said, many times.

'OK Mrs K?' we said in unison.

'Girls!' she said, panting. 'Girls. This lift. How do you survive it?' She asked between breaths. 'I came out ten minutes ago, and I'm suffering. I need breeze. Your dad must fix. Get some air in there. This lift is Satan's sauna, I tell you.'

'You've been here ten minutes, Mrs K?' I said. Phone poised. 'Did you hear anything down there on The Tri?'

'Yes, I heard you crying and running, but you two are always sprinting and making noise. What happened now?'

I looked at Norva. I didn't know what to say.

I didn't want to confirm it. I shouldn't have brought it up.

Norva jumped in. 'Ah, you know how it goes, Mrs K. Hormones.'

'Ah yes, I remember those,' she replied with a smile.

'We just went to Art Club, but Hugo wasn't there. When did you see him last?' I asked, taking back the conversation.

The investigation had officially commenced. Norva smiled encouragingly at me.

Mrs Kowalski looked into the sky, recalling her thoughts. 'I saw him Friday at the meeting. Bad meeting,' she said darkly. 'After that – I talked with Sissy. She does not stop talking! Wow.'

'And after Sissy?' Norva asked.

'After Sissy, I got home and waited for a friend to help me with my project,' Mrs K said quietly.

'Who?' I said. 'Which project?'

'You two are so nosy!'

Mrs Kowalski staggered to her flat, saying what I believed to be very rude Polish words with every step.

Norva fished for her keys in her bag.

'Ringlet?' she trilled, way too close to my ear.

The door swung open.

I strongly disliked that dog. I pushed her into the flat, irritated.

Ringo was in our room, of course. Sitting on my bed, naturally. His back legs angled at 90 degrees as he licked at his most private of parts.

Ringo looked up at us, sighed and went back to his meal. His life unchanged, completely unaware that Hugo had gone.

Norva went to grab Ringo with a kiss. He sniffed at her and recoiled, twisting himself from her arms. His fur stuck to her sweaty jaw, giving her a thin, Santa-like beard.

I smiled.

'Laugh it up, you deserve it today,' Norva said, wiping her face.

Norva undressed, leaving her clothes in a puddle where she stood.

I silently gazed across the Tri from the large window opposite our beds. A view Hugo would no longer see. I took a seat at our desk and booted up the computer.

While it took a frankly despicable long time to load, I thought about a title for the document. Finally, I typed: `hugo_down.doc`

11

'I'm almost too hot to function, Nik.' Norva whimpered. She star-fished on her bed, in her towel.

'I can't deal with this heat.'

'I need you to deal. Please,' I replied. 'We have to solve this quickly. For Hugo, for all of us.'

'Oh, don't you worry, I said *almost* function. I'm ready. I live for this. I'm just baking like a potato over here,' she said. 'Plus, I was consulting my waters.'

'Well, while you were doing that,' I began. 'I located some sections of the 2006 edition of the Murder …'

'… Investigation Manual!' Norva squealed, finishing my sentence.

I nodded.

'My incomplete bible,' she said solemnly.

'You remember the building blocks of an investigation?' I asked.

'But of course.'

Norva sat up, and paced up and down in front of the window. She held a fan in front of her face.

'Keep the victim alive – it's way too late for that,' she said.

I looked away, and sighed.

'Sorry. Sorry. The next one is "keep the scene on lockdown." Hmm, that's going to be tricky.'

'Yes, I don't know about that.'

'Then you've got,' Norva took a deep breath, 'snatch evidence, name victim and point fingers. Open the doc. I'm ready to get into it.'

'Me too,' I said. My fingers poised above the keyboard.

'The victim is identified,' she said flatly.

I nodded.

Victim: Hugo Knightley-Webb

'Time of death?'

'`Tri_thoughts` and `Bedroom_Window_logs` – and the smell you smelled – point to Friday night, early Saturday morning.' I said flicking through my phone. 'Plus, Sissy, Barry and Mrs Kowalski just confirmed they haven't seen him since the meeting. You know, the meeting we should have been at, Norva.'

I glared at Norva as she looked out of the window.

'Alright, alright, we'll get to that. Note the times, will you?'

`Time of death: Between Fri 20/07 22:30 and Sat 06:30`

'We need to narrow that down. Add that to our to-dos.'

'Done.'

`To-do: Close the time of death window`

'Cause of death?' I asked.

Norva spun around to face me. 'It's not obvious to you? Paint can to the brain, wrapped in a Tri bag and chucked down the chute!'

'Wait a minute, Norva, we need to unpack that...'

'Be my guest. The floor is yours,' she said, taking a bow.

'OK, the paint can,' I started. 'It did have blood, and what I positively identified to be Hugo's hair on it, so that's looking likely.'

'Add it.'

Weapon: Paint can

'He was definitely in a Tri bag. Confirmed. Pap and Mark have access to those – and the paint.'

'Wait, wait, wait – so you think Mark and or Pap did it?' Norva said, her eyes wide. She flapped her hand in front of her face. 'Oh my god, oh my god, oh my god.'

'Norva, hold on. Facts, evidence, deduction. Let's ask them who might have access to those and how…' I looked away towards the screen. 'Because I'm pretty certain no one else does. That will help us narrow down the potential suspects.'

To-do: Ask Pap about the paint/bags

Norva gulped and nodded. 'OK, and the chute? What's your beef with the chute?'

'I have no 'beef' with the chute, it's called

being thorough,' I said. 'Just because he's in the bins under it, doesn't mean he came through it. He could have been put in the bins directly.'

'Doubt it,' said Norva with a snort. 'Hugo was a hench, heavy man when he was alive; imagine his weight in dead mode!'

I winced.

Norva noticed.

'Sorry, insensitive. You'd have to be pretty strong to carry him far. Why would you risk that? Dragging a corpse around the Tri? Especially when the lifts were broken – and broken during his time of death window? Ain't having it.'

'Point made,' I said. 'But do you think Hugo – being so large and heavy – could even fit in the chute?'

'Only one way to find out,' she said with a smile. 'To be tested – once we've finished this little meet up.' She fluttered her hand at me.

To-do: Test The Hugo/Chute hypothesis

'So that bring us to the suspects,' I said. Do you have an idea of who it could be?

Norva turned to face the window.

'My waters AND bones are telling me it's someone in this Corner, you know. Has to be. If Hugo's body has come from the Corner One, Third Avenue chute, which I'm convinced it did. You can straight up discount Corners Two and Three – they use their own chutes, and the Avenues connecting the buildings haven't been safe to walk on for like years now.'

This was true – the safety aspect, but not the time line. The walkways connecting the buildings had been condemned for eight months.

I flicked back through the photographs folder on my phone. Images of Norva at either end of each Avenue, making peace signs. Warning signs, telling residents to 'KEEP OFF', clearly behind her.

The photographs were dated February 13.

'What floors are those chutes on again?'

'7, 14 and 21,' I confirmed.

'There's a chute on each Avenue right, the walkways?'

I nodded.

'In our little area,' Norva waved her hand in a large circle. 'Only our floor – 22 – and the one below – 21 – use that chute, right?'

I searched 'avenues' in `Tri_Thoughts.doc` and confirmed the trend.

'Yes, Floors 21 and 22,' I said. "Floor 20 and below take the lift on floor 14 to Second Avenue, if they want to use a chute. This makes the lifts stink.'

Norva spun around.

'And. The. Lifts. Were. Broken. On. Friday. Night!' Norva said, clapping with each word.

She smiled and took another little bow.

'You know, I'm ready to call it. Lemme go in. Hugo died in the murderer's flat. One of six,' she said. 'Put these in.'

I typed as Norva spoke.

'From the top: Floor 22. Me, you, Pap…'

We stared at each other. Norva shook the thought away. 'And The Ringlet.'

She reached down to stroke Ringo.

He immediately turned over and offered his stomach.

'Ole Girl, Mrs K. Mark and his mother,' she sighed and looked to the sky, wistfully. She continued, 'Then, below on 21, where the avenue is: Jane, the money-raiser. My chum and his mum. Hugo and his sister.'

I changed those words to proper nouns and added them to a fresh table.

I included some prompts for us to follow.

'Anyone we can rule out at this stage?' I asked.

Norva looked at me with a serious face.

'Well did you do it, Nik? Did you? I need to be certain. Facts. Evidence. Deduction and all that,' she said, mocking me. 'Just saying.'

'Did you do it, Norva?' I said with a sigh.

'Don't answer a question with a question!'

'No, I didn't do it. I was – unfortunately – watching *Death in Paradise* with you.'

I scrolled through my phone.

'According to Tri_thoughts.doc, we went to bed at 22:15. You snored, until you walked Ringo on Saturday morning.'

I showed her my phone. 'Here's a photo of you with your mouth wide open at 01:27. I slept until 01:25. I checked my phone when…'

I paused.

'When what?' Norva questioned.

'When Pap came home.'

Silence.

Norva coughed to break it. 'He could have been anywhere. What happened next?'

'I took that photo of you, and went back to sleep. I heard nothing until you woke me up. Facts. Evidence. Deduction.'

'Good,' she said with a slight smile. 'Well, you can officially remove us, then – and RingRing – as suspects. Plus, how we could handle that hefty body discreetly, I don't know.'

Norva looked around the room. 'Mark's mum's been bed-bound since her accident, so she didn't do it. And I very highly doubt Hugo climbed into a bag and launched himself down the chute, so rule him out while you're at it.'

She reached for her sandals. 'Let's move – grab some bin bags and some books,' she said.

'Wait,' I said, holding out my hand. 'There's more to discuss, Norva. Potential motives?'

'True, true. We'll get to that. We need to pound the pavement for that intel, though. Also – who was that 'friend' Mrs K mentioned she was with? A project? In the middle of the night? Pffft! Shady. We also need to know where everyone else was at,' Norva said, standing in the doorway.

'Especially Pap, Norva,' I said. 'We need to speak to him as a priority. Something serious happened between him and Hugo at the meeting – everyone's talking about it and soon they'll be talking to the police. We need the details.'

Norva nodded. I continued.

'Also – who was he speaking to when we told him about Hugo just now? What about his limp? How long has he had that, where did it come fr…'

'Nik!' Norva jumped in with a laugh. A forced and faked laugh. 'Pap can speak to who he pleases, and his limp has nothing to do with the price of fish has it? Is he officially your main suspect? You think he did it?'

I was quiet.

'Of course, I don't think he did it, Norva. But someone else might.'

Hugo_down_2307.doc

Victim: Hugo Knightley-Webb
Body location: Corner One Refuse Area
Date and Time of discovery: 23/07 14:27

Time of death: Between Fri 20/07 22:30 and
Sat 06:30
Weapon: Paint can

Hypothesis: Murdered in Corner One flat, either
floor 21 or 22, with paint can, placed in chute

To-do: Find out about the meeting
To-do: Find out where the suspects went after
the meeting
To-do: Ask Pap about his conversation and
limp
To-do: Test The Hugo/chute hypothesis
To-do: Ask Pap about the paint/bags
To-do: Close the time of death window

	221 Pap ~~Nik~~ ~~Noeva~~ ~~Ringo~~	222 Mrs Kowalski	223 Mark Walker ~~Mother Walker~~	211 George Shah Nina Shah	212 ~~Hugo KW~~ Serena KW	213 Charity Jane
Suspect's alibi during TOD window	Out until 01:27	Working on a project with 'a friend'.				
Corroborated?						
Motivation?						
Questions?						

12

'Quick – while, I'm doing this, check under the sink for those bags, yeah? Pap might have 'liberated' a few for himself,' Norva said, as she rifled through Pap's wardrobe.

Good point. I was certain I'd seen a few Tri bags in there.

I stepped out of Pap's room, back into the hall and paced down the short hallway through the living room and into the kitchen. I sat on my knees and pulled the doors under the sink open.

- washing powder
- shoe polish
- rubber gloves

Where were they? I reached further into the cupboard, blindly.

- dishcloths
- miscellaneous rags
- Heavy-duty Tri bags

'Found them!' I shouted into the hall. No reply.

I snatched them triumphantly and ran back to Pap's room. No Norva. I turned around to face our room and jumped back, surprised.

Norva stood in the doorway silently, with her head cocked to the left.

'Is this Hugo's vibe?' she said brightly. She held up a pair of Pap's old jeans and a never-worn long-sleeved checked shirt against her body.

'What do you reckon? Would he go for this?'

'Norva, does it even matter?' I said exasperated. 'It'll do. It's only a temporary measure.'

'I'm just trying to do your boy justice, you know – dignity in death and that.'

I stared at her.

'You're right, you're right. I'm sorry. Let's crack on – the cops will be crawling all over the scene like me on Mark in my dreams any second now.'

I threw up in my mouth, a little.

We had gathered quite the range of household items to make 'the 'body'.

- books
- black tape
- candles
- quilts
- old school trophies
- our old clothes

We stuffed it all into Pap's clothing. Pap was tall, like Hugo, but much leaner. We wrapped the shirt and jeans in black tape to secure their contents.

Norva poked our chute-test dummy with her foot.

'I don't know about you, Hugo Too. You don't look very...human.' She attempted to lift up our crudely taped prop. She strained. 'And you're heavy, but not stressfully so.'

I looked at our misshapen invention.

'It's not just about the weight, necessarily. It's the size, remember? Will he actually fit in the chute?'

'You tell me, Nik,' Norva said. 'Of the two of us, you were closer to him. What's your verdict?'

I leaned in.

The height was right. The shoulder width, not so much. I pulled at the neck of the shirt, and stuffed two scrunched pillowcases into each armhole.

'Looks good, sis,' said Norva. 'Hugo would be crazy proud of that. He'd get that in the Tate Modern, no doubt.'

It did look better, and that made me feel worse. I turned my back on Norva and blinked my tears away.

'Let's do it,' I said, turning on my heel and unfurling the roll of Tri bags.

Norva smiled gently at me. 'That's the spirit.'

Into the bag 'he' went.

13

We slowly opened the front door and peered out into the hallway. The coast was clear.

Norva stepped out to double check. She swung her head dramatically from side to side.

'Come through,' she stage whispered. I pulled on the bag, and immediately pulled a muscle around my ribs. I winced.

'Deal with it,' she said without a single trace of sympathy.

Norva jumped through the doorway to push the bag from the other side. She closed and locked the door behind her. We passed Mrs Kowalski's. We passed Mark's.

We made it to the lift. Floor 22 complete, floor 21 to go.

Norva reached for the call button.

'Don't,' I said quietly. 'It was broken on Friday, remember? We take the stairs.'

'I don't want to, though. Eurgh, do I have to?' she whined. 'It stinks.'

I nodded. 'Move.'

We opened the door to the stairwell and were immediately greeted by the familiar stench of stale pee. After exchanging glances we attempted to carry the body down the staircase.

The bag hit every step on the way down.

It was a strong bag, but it couldn't withstand the constant scraping against the concrete. It began to split; as it did, a rubber gloved 'hand' popped out.

Instant, stinging flashback to Hugo's ringed fingers. I blinked away hot tears.

'Oh my days, Hugo Too, forgive us,' Norva said, noticing the glove. 'It's like you're been murdered all over again.'

It was.

It was disrespectful.

It was also the right thing to do.

Now I knew Norva was correct. Transporting a body any further than this was too risky. Too hard. Too heavy. Whoever did this, did this nearby. And that was terrifying.

As I reached out to push the door to floor 21, it suddenly opened in front of me. Mark stood there chewing, looking up at us. A bottle of Vitonica in his right hand. A burger in his left. I slammed my back against the wall.

Norva was rooted to the spot. She dropped her end of the bag immediately.

40% fear. 60% love struck.

'Alright?' Mark muttered, his mouth full.

He nodded, walked past me and began to take the stairs to the floor above.

The door swung shut behind him.

He looked down at the fake body. I stepped in front the bag to somewhat conceal it.

Fail.

'Wassat?' he asked, pointing.

Norva was silent.

I coughed.

I clearly had to deal with this. 'We're having a tidy up.'

'Looks like a body in there, HA!' Mark laughed loudly. I could see his lunch in his mouth. 'Better stay away from you two!'

'Y-you don't have to do that,' Norva said meekly behind me, suddenly finding her voice.

'Does it look like a body? Really? I wouldn't know,' I asked Mark, faking sweetness, feeling brave. 'What do you know about dead bodies?'

Mark suddenly stopped laughing. 'Nothing. Nothing at all.' He walked up the stairs.

I shouted after him. 'How comes you're on floor 21, Mark? Is the lift broken again?'

I knew it wasn't.

'Ah, I don't, I don't think so,' he said. He stumbled over his words. 'I-I just popped into Serena's. Went to get a juice. Quicker than going to Better Buy. Also, free from the source.'

He shook the bottle near Norva's face with a smile and he continued up the stairs, biting his burger as he went.

I pushed the door and walked out on to Third Avenue.

'A little help, next time?'

'Don't crush shame me, OK? When I'm near him, I can't function. One day you'll understand.'

'I highly doubt that,' I said. 'Open the chute.'

The entrance to the chute, was black approximately a metre square; the bottom reached my waist, making it around 50 centimetres from the ground.

Norva pulled the handle, and it opened easily.

The smell of death wafted up. I couldn't look down. I bit my lip.

'Right, grab your end, Norva,' I said, readying myself. 'I'll angle the head. Don't, I repeat, DO NOT push or let go. This is just to see if he fits. Then we dismantle him and get…'

'Yeah I know, I know!' Norva broke in, rolling her eyes. 'I know what I'm doing…'

'OH MY DAYS!' A voice – screamed – behind us.

Stunned, I jumped, and let go of the head.

Startled, Norva shrieked, and let go of the legs.

The 'body' slid down the chute. Gone. The bag loudly hit the skip at the other end.

To-do: Test The Hugo/Chute hypothesis

Norva and I stared at each other, turning to the source of the scream. George.

'What in fresh hell are you loons up to now? Why you so jumpy?'

'Oh my god! Oh my god! Oh my god!' Norva shouted, staring at me eyes wide with panic. 'There are gonna be two more murders when this is exposed. Why did you let go? What's wrong with *you*?'

68

'What's wrong with *me*?' I said. '*You* let go too!' My stomach burned. 'Oh this is bad, this doesn't help Pap in any way.'

'We've got to get Hugo Too back!'

'You don't say,' I said flatly.

'Yo, NSquared!' George shouted, interupting us. 'Murders? Get who back? You wanna clue me in or nah?'

'You'll know in about five minutes, mate,' Norva sighed. 'It's really bad this time.' She turned to me. 'Extra bad, now.'

Sirens suddenly rang out below.

14

'Yo, you are lying! Tell me you're lying?'

George's hand flew to his mouth.

'No way...' He stared at Norva, blinking in shock. 'For real?'

I nodded.

'And you were seeing if he could fit in the chute? I mashed up your reconstruction?'

Norva nodded.

'I cannot believe Hugo is dead, man,' George said with a sigh. 'And I'm sorry for freaking you out.' He shook his head at the lift's floor. 'I cannot believe you two are so on it, though. You legit detectives now? What is life?'

'I know,' I said. 'But being right this time is, well, so wrong.'

'I don't feel 'wrong' to be honest,' said Norva. 'I'm in this now and we're way ahead of the cops. We know how they did it; the suspects … are narrowed down.'

'You got names in the frame?' said George, eyes wide. 'NSquared, you're rapid. Who's made the list?'

'Well,' I said quietly. 'Where were you on Friday night, after the meeting?'

George roared with laughter. 'Come on now, bald one. Look at me. I'm not about that murder life. I was out. I was…'

The lift opened on the ground floor.

A crowd had gathered in the lobby, and it spilled outside and around the refuse area. Residents talked to each other in loud and confused voices.

'Oh no,' I said. 'Our retrieval mission is going to prove impossible.'

Norva's eyes scanned the crowd.

'Wow,' shouted George over the noise. 'This is officially crazy.' He held up the waist of his sagging jeans and jumped up three times. 'Oop – there's my mum, gotta fill her in on the madness.'

George pushed through the crowd. 'I'll catch you up. In a bit!' he shouted back at us.

'That there was so smooth, Nik. Real slick.'
Norva shook her head at me.

'What?' I said loudly. 'Which bit?'

'Shussssh! George's alibi,' she said in a low
voice.

'What?' I repeated, quieter this time. 'We needed his alibi so we could rule him out.'

'Yeah, I know that, Officer Obvious,' she said.
'But you can use a bit of flair, a bit of style. Dial back
the blunt. Also, we know full well that George ain't the
one. He's not out here, moving bodies. Like us.'

'Not funny, but yes, it's unlikely,' I agreed. 'Our
– botched – experiment just proved that one adolescent
couldn't handle the weight. But we need to know for
sure. Anyway,' I said. 'That's not a priority. Let's figure
out how we're going to get the body back and potentially spot our suspects.'

'Yas!' Norva said. 'Multitasking! Let's see
if they're being shady. You know, crims often come
back to their scenes. Scope out the vibe, get some
thrills.'

'That's weird.'

'People are weird,' she replied.

Norva pushed through the crowd. People
tutted and kissed their teeth as she barged past.

I walked in her wake, offering meek apologies on her behalf, keeping my eye on the refuse area.

Bad news.

A lone, thin Policeman, had begun setting up a perimeter. Blue and white crime-scene tape gently fluttered around it.

'Iconic,' Norva whispered.

The policeman looked down at his watch and sighed. He looked back at the growing crowd.

'How are we going to get around this, Norva?' I asked. 'And him?'

'I'm working it out,' she replied. Her eyes narrowed and she scanned the area. 'He's the only one here – we have time.'

'You sure?'

'I mean, no, not at all, but what else can we do right now? Let's park it here for a moment. This is a hot scoping spot.'

Pap stood next to the Policeman and together they blocked the entrance to the refuse area. Eager residents craned their necks for a gruesome glimpse.

One person was shouting [Barry from Bermuda's]. Three people were shaking their heads. One person was crying softly. Five people were talking on their phones. Another was trying to take a video.

'Ghouls,' Norva said. 'Now, where are our suspects?'

I scanned the crowd. George had his arm around his mother, Nina. She was crying and jabbing out a message on her phone. He noticed us, shook his head, and threw his hands up at the scene.

Charity Jane approached Pap. She offered a sympathetic smile and squeezed his hand. She stood close to him. Their arms touched.

'Why do you think Jane's up there?' I asked Norva.

'She's 'nice,' remember? Gaga for goodwill. Putting on a front, by standing at the front. Gets her up in everyone's business, 24-7. Plus, she's getting a good old scope of the scene, I bet.'

I reached for my phone and took a photo.

'Oh wow!' whispered Norva, gripping my arm.

'What? What now? I asked, on high alert.

'Oh god, he's behind us!'

'Who?' I asked.

Norva stood taller and touched her braids.

Stupid questions. It was Mark.

I looked back at him. He surveyed the scene, mouth agape, eyes narrowed.

Norva slipped away from me. She walked in a

circle around him, three times. Stomach in, chest out, hoping he'd notice her.

He didn't.

I watched him, watching the scene. Mark looked genuinely shocked. His eyes darted around the crowd. Searching for someone.

'What's up, Joe? It's Hugo? Whappen? He dead?' someone shouted in my ear behind us, as they pushed to the front. Residents emerged from the Corners, from The Rec, from Better Buy, from Bermuda's.

We stepped forward out of their way. A couple stood next to us were deep in conversation. Low voices. Corner Threes.

'You hear about Joe and Hugo's run in on Friday?'

'Hear about it? I was there, mate. It was wild − Joe went *off*!'

I strained to hear, and nudged Norva. Someone to our left pushed us into the couple. Their voices trailed away as they noticed Norva and me observing them − through narrowed eyes. They shrugged and disappeared into the throng.

Pap's name was circulating as a suspect. Fact. I looked at Norva. She refused to meet my eyes, and instead stared ahead into the crowd.

Her nose wrinkled.

'What's that smell?'

Mrs Kowalski ambled past, a platter of pierogis in her hand.

We were in no mood to eat. Others were though. They snatched the food, snacking while the scene unfolded. Mrs K smiled at us and shrugged.

'Pierogi is the new popcorn, eh girls?' she said as she moved away.

'She remains a suspect,' I said to Norva under my breath. 'Her behaviour is too odd. How could you be so cheerful at a time like this?'

'Hmmm,' Norva nodded. 'And handing out snacks? It's like she's being too obvious, so we won't suspect her. She's trying to bluff. Too late, Kowalski, you're already on the list. We see you.'

I glanced at Pap and Jane. They spoke quietly together. Jane's eyes were wet. She dabbed at them constantly with the heel of her hand. The policeman stared straight ahead.

A sudden loud sob from behind us made me jump.

'No!' The familiar voice screamed. 'No!'

The crowd parted.

Serena pushed her way to the front. She clawed at the crime scene tape. Ripped it down and threw it to the ground. Pap lurched forward to grab her. She shrieked loudly, a wounded animal in intense pain.

Serena stared at Pap. He nodded and she burst into tears and collapsed into him. He comforted her, burying her head into his shoulders. He stroked her hair tenderly.

My stomach burned for her and her loss. Tears formed in my eyes.

Charity Jane looked uncomfortable. She looked at Pap and Serena. Sadness tinged with frustration. Jane spotted us and quickly turned away from our gaze, she stepped away and disappeared into the crowd.

'A sharp exit,' murmured Norva. 'Seeing the victim's family was too much, eh. Too real?'

Blue lights flashed across our faces. Additional Police. A single, siren-less car rolled into the Tri. Once it came to a halt, a young Policewoman stepped out, straightening her hat.

Norva squinted and pointed.

'Yes, it's Katie! This is it. Let's move.'

We reached the perimeter at the same time. Pap waved at her, and Katie raised her hand in reply. Serena's face remained buried in Pap's chest.

'Katie!' Norva said, stepping in front of her. 'Katie, we're so glad you're here!'

'Girls! Girls!' she said, hugging us. 'Hugo!' she whispered. 'I can't believe it. I just can't believe it. You found him, I heard?' She shook her head, and squeezed us harder, her eyes welling with tears. 'I'm so, so sorry.'

'We're sorry, too,' I said. 'It's terrible. We're glad you're here.'

'Yeah?' she laughed bitterly, letting us out her embrace, wiping her eyes. 'A bit of classified information for you – I'm terrified, honestly. I shouldn't say that out loud, should I? This is major. So major. I'm so nervous. I think I've forgotten most of my training and…'

'No, you haven't' said Norva. 'You've got this. We know you. We'll help.'

Katie stood up to her full height, which admittedly wasn't very tall. 5'3". Same as me. She was suddenly stern. She looked into our eyes.

'Girls, no. No, no, no. That's not what I meant at all – it wasn't an invitation.' She cursed herself under her breath. 'You must stay out of this one. This is not a game. I need you out of it. I can do this. I can. I think?'

'Officer Smyth, when you're ready please?' A voice coughed behind us. The thin Policeman.

Katie spun around. 'Yes!' she replied loudly, 'Yes, Officer Burnett.' Quieter now. 'I'm, um, working on community relations,' she said, looking back at us with a weak smile.

'Good for you,' he snapped back, sarcastically. 'I've been the only one at the scene for altogether too long. I need you to take over the cordon and reset the tape. The victim's sister,' he jerked a thumb towards Serena, 'ripped it down.' He sighed. 'I need to set up the Major Investigation Room.'

Officer Burnett thrust a piece of paper into her hand.

'What's this?' Katie asked him.

'What's this!?' He replied incredulously. 'That's the crime scene log, Kathryn. Remember those? From your training?'

The situation was incredibly awkward. Norva raised an eyebrow. Katie was embarrassed. Her cheeks flushed.

'Yes, yes, of course. Yes.' Katie stared intensely at the log. 'OK, so no one's touched the scene yet?' she asked.

'Of course not!' He snapped. 'We have to wait

for a strategy from the Senior Investigating Officer. I just set the cordon.' Officer Burnett looked out across the crowd. 'Speaking of which, where are they? Who's been assigned? Where is everyone else?'

'I don't know, ' said Katie without looking up.

15

The radio attached to Officer Burnett's vest buzzed to life.

'Mike Bravo five, Mike Bravo five, this is Sierra Juliet two-one. Over.'

He grabbed the radio and turned his back to us. Katie leaned towards him, listening in.

'Sierra Juliet two-one, this is Mike Bravo five. Go ahead. Over.'

We strained to hear the message. We could barely understand it, which was obviously the point.

'Mike Bravo, an SIO has been assigned to your incident. Detective Chief Inspector Sharp has an ETA of ten, I repeat, ten minutes. Delay due to a developing Code thirteen in Highbury. Officers across all boroughs are being briefed and diverted to that situation. Over.'

Officer Burnett sucked in a breath through his teeth and shook his head before returning to the call.

'Sierra Juliet two-one. Received. Out.' The radio was silent. He clipped it back into his vest.

'DCI Sharp…' said Katie.

'The one and only,' replied Officer Burnett. 'If she sees the state of this cordon, there's going to be hell to pay. I need your focus on this, Officer Smyth! Now.'

Burnett thrust a roll of blue and white tape into her hand. She quickly walked away, unfurling the tape, the crime scene log tucked under her arm.

He turned to us. 'You two need to move back, and go home.' He shouted over us: 'Everyone, back away; please leave the scene. Please leave the scene…'

The crowd listened and began to disperse. Slowly.

'Take her home? We'll be up to talk with you further shortly,' said Officer Burnett to Pap.

Pap nodded and with his arm around Serena, walked towards the lobby. He looked at us, and mouthed, 'Let's go.'

We nodded, but we weren't going anywhere. Norva reached for her phone and thumbed out a quick message.

'Who are you texting now!' I demanded.

'A decoy,' she laughed.

A decoy?

Ding! Ding!

An instant reply. We stepped away as people streamed past us.

'What's happening North of the river?' Norva wondered. 'Sounds epic. I'm pretty sure 'Code thirteen' is a major incident, and I…'

'Norva, we don't have the capacity to think about that; we have our own major incident here, remember? And by the sound of it, this DCI Sharp person isn't going to be enthused about us rifling through their crime scene. A plan? Now? We've got ten minutes!'

'I know,' said Norva, looking around the scene. 'I'm fully aware. I'm on it. Plus, no one's been in there yet – you heard Katie. We have a little time.'

Officer Burnett strode past, to our left, heading towards the lobby.

'Perfect,' she said, walking over to Katie.

'Katie, the cordon looks great – good job,' said Norva, smiling. She lightly touched the blue tape, and then stretched it in her hands.

Katie smiled back, 'Thanks, but you need to go now. Really. DCI Sharp is, well, she's no joke, and I need to be ready to brief her.'

'We totally understand, one more thing…' Norva began, while backing away. Before she finished, loud, booming sirens rang out across The Tri.

16

George ran towards the cordon with a large speaker in his arms.

'Katie!' he screamed over the 'music'. 'Yas, you're home, Officer Official!' He dropped the speaker by her feet and a confused Katie covered her ears.

'I made this track just for you! Specifically for your comeback.' He grinned wildly. 'Do you love it or nah?'

'George, what the hell are you doing…?' she began to shout, as George quickly drew her into an all consuming bear hug.

He towered over her, pushing her head into his chest, swaying with her from side to side. Katie struggled in his arms.

George looked over at us and nodded, his eyes wild and wide.

Our sign from our decoy.

Norva nodded in return and grabbed my hand. We ran under the cordon and pushed the doors to the refuse area.

Inside, I panted and held my chest. And then my nose.

'Norva, oh my god...I...'

'No time, no time,' said Norva between tight lips. 'Grab him and tear him apart.'

The music continued loudly outside.

Fortunately, 'he' was hanging on the side of the bin, freed from his bag. Together, we pulled him onto the floor. I daren't look back into the bin. I couldn't.

Hugo, I'm sorry about this. All of this.

'Nik! Concentrate, yeah? Just get the stuff out, and scatter it, OK?'

'OK'

We ripped at the body like feral foxes. The most surreal moment of my life. I was certainly having some kind of out-of-body experience.

'Why did we use so much tape on you Hugo Too? Why!' said Norva, snapping me back to reality.

Whatever 'reality' was at this point. I wasn't sure.

'Here we go!' she exclaimed as we broke through the tape.

Out came the items.

'Goodbye trophies, goodbye books. Goodbye Pap's new shirt – we hardly knew you,' Norva said, as she garnished the room with our belongings.

She turned to me. 'I think we're done here.'

I nodded.

We stood by the door and Norva pushed it open slightly. We peered through the gap.

The music boomed in front of us. George gesticulated wildly at the speaker, pretending he didn't know how to turn it off. Katie stood in front of him, her hands covering her ears.

'Now!' said Norva. We sprang from the refuse room, and ran to the cordon.

I ducked under the tape, but Norva snatched at it, as she came through. It fluttered to the ground.

She reached for my hand and pulled me towards George and Katie. As I covered my ears, Norva nodded at George, and she crouched in front of the speaker. She prodded a button and the music stopped.

'Thank YOU!' someone shouted from above. It was followed by a smattering of applause.

'What the hell is going on here?' A voice boomed from behind.

17

'What kind of goddamn cordon is this, Officer Smyth?'
DCI Sharp demanded with a low snarl.

Katie froze.

Black cotton trousers, white silk vest, greying afro
hair. DCI Sharp reached down, picking up the broken
tape on the floor. She threw it at Katie's feet.

'Where's Officer Burnett?' she snapped.

'Setting up the Investigation Room, DCI Sharp,'
Katie replied. She glanced at us, a warning to move
away with one look. We understood.

Norva, George and I began to slink backwards,
away from the wrath. Too late. Spotted. Her eyes fixed
on us.

'And who are you? Why the noise?'

'So, like, see what had happened was…' began George, pointing towards the speaker.

Katie broke in, 'DCI Sharp, forgive the distraction, I was developing community relations, and…'

'*Developing community relations*?' DCI Sharp said incredulously. 'By having a rave at a crime scene?'

'Barely a rave…' remarked George.

DCI Sharp threw him the iciest of looks. He caught it and immediately fell silent.

'Pick up your stereo, and go,' she said quietly.

As George bent over to grab the speaker, DCI Sharp groaned. 'Oh god, what are *they* doing here already?'

We turned around. As the sun had begun to go down, the journalists turned up. A Cloud News van crawled into the Tri. The crew jumped out with their cameras, their lights and their furry microphones on sticks. They set up camp next to the cordon, looking for the perfect shot. The perfect soundbite.

May Burton, 56. Cloud News reporter − professional story distorter − stepped out of the van, surveying the scene. She spotted DCI Sharp, chuckled to herself and walked over.

'May,' DCI Sharp said tersely, staring into her eyes.

'Alice,' the journalist replied, holding her gaze. First name terms. 'We meet again. It's been too long.'

Their reunion was quickly interrupted.

'Do one!' shouted a resident from above. 'You only turn up to share bad news. Making us look bad!' Boos rained down from across the Tri.

Others weren't so negative though. They began queuing to be on camera, to enjoy a fleeting moment of fame. DCI Sharp returned to the scene and May moved towards the camera. Their natural habitats.

Norva and I loitered behind, casual and inconspicuous, naturally – hoping to hear something useful for the files.

As George began to walk away with the speaker, Norva whispered: 'Oh my god, thank you so much!'

'Any time, NSquared, I got you,' he said in a low voice. 'But you owe me big. Huge!'

'Thanks, George!' I said. 'You saved us.'

'You mean I saved us,' said Norva. 'I'm the mastermind.'

'Can you carry on your inane conversation elsewhere?' May Burton snapped at us. 'You're blocking my light!'

We shifted to the left, Norva shooting her dirty looks with each side step.

'Ferals,' May muttered under her breath, smoothed her brown bobbed hair and patted down her skirt suit in preparation for her first interviewee. A make-up artist rushed forward to powder her nose. May tilted her head towards the woman gratefully and then quickly shoved her away. 'Enough!' she growled.

Barry stepped forward. 'Ready for my close-up, May,' he slurred loudly with a laugh.

A wide man holding the microphone, wearing headphones, recoiled and rolled his eyes.

May Burton snapped into TV mode. She pressed her earpiece with her left hand.

'Yes, yes, that's right, Peter,' she replied to the person presumably back in the studio. 'I'm at the scene with Barry West, landlord of the local pub, Bermuda's. So tell us about the victim, Barry? What was he like?' she asked.

'The victim? His name was Hugo, and he was a great guy. Good people! Gin and slim, he drank. Ordered it every time. Twist of lime. Zesty man. Fun! Talked a lot. Arty farty.' Barry waved his hand around. 'Rich. Money money monneeeey. Must be funnnnnny,' he sang into the microphone, laughing.

'This is the hottest of messes,' Norva muttered.

May interrupted, attempting to take control of the 'interview'.

'So, Hugo was wealthy, Barry? A wealthy man, living here, on the Tri?' she snorted incredulously.

The wide man holding the microphone shook his head with dismay.

'No offence!' she laughed.

'Fake,' said Norva, under her breath.

From the corner of my eye, I could see Pap walking towards us. He mouthed, 'Let's go.' He jerked his thumb towards the lobby.

'Did Hugo have any enemies here? Anyone who would murder him, Barry?' May asked.

I shook my head at Pap. We're not leaving now. This was just getting interesting.

'Enemies? Nah, no. Not Hugo,' he said.

Barry looked past the camera and noticed Pap. Oh no. My heart met my mouth.

'Oh, wait, except Joe here,' he pointed at Pap.

There it was. We should have left. We should have gone! My stomach flipped. I stared at Norva. She glared at Barry. Her chest rose and fell with anger.

I looked at Pap. His eyes were wide. His hands shook. DCI Sharp was listening, and staring at Pap.

'Come on up, Joe!' Barry said, stepping out of shot, pulling Pap towards him. 'You all heard Joe threatened Hugo on Friday? At the meeting about that statue? Was the talk of Bermuda's. Well, until this.'

May and her team turned towards us. She opened her mouth to speak.

'No comment,' shouted Pap before her words arrived. He pulled us away from the scene and limped angrily to the lobby.

Norva and I followed quickly behind him, exchanging terrified looks. My heart and mind raced. An accusation! On live television. On Cloud News? With the DCI Sharp watching. The very definition of a situation escalating quickly.

Pap repeatedly pressed the call button, looking over his shoulder the entire time.

We rode the lift in shocked silence, not knowing where to look, unable to meet each other's eyes.

18

Pap put his key in our front door but it swung open without resistance. Strange.

We locked that door. 100%.

Norva looked at me with wide, confused eyes and gripped Pap's arm.

A figure stood silently in the hallway.

'No! NO! We don't want to die!' I screamed.

I ducked down behind Pap.

Norva dug her nails deep into his bicep, shrieking directly into his right ear. Pap shook Norva off him, irritated and in pain.

'Calm down, I know who that is,' he said, exasperatedly holding the side of his face, shaking his arm.

'I-I'm so sorry! I didn't mean to scare you!' the voice said, meekly.

Charity Jane.

Dad slapped at the hallway light switch.

'How the hell did you get in, Jane?' Norva shouted, squinting in the light. She breathed heavily.

'How did you know who that was, in the dark, Pap?' I wondered, out loud.

Jane looked nervous. She tucked her hair behind her ear. Her bottom lip trembled. She stared at Pap. She pointed at the door. 'It was unlocked.'

Lies. It wasn't. No way.

Norva stared at me. She ran her index finger across her neck, pointed at her eyes and then at Jane. Norva was very subtle and discrete.

Jane burst into a flood of tears. 'I'm absolutely terrified, Joe!'

'Yeah, well that makes four of us, Jane,' Norva said.

Pap shook his head, and gingerly touched Jane's shoulder.

'I've brought sandwiches,' she said, brightening up.

'Thank you,' he said with a slightly irritated sigh. He walked Jane through the lounge into the kitchen.

They talked in hushed voices. Norva and I faced each other in the hallway.

'Norva?' I whispered hoarsely. 'Cloud News, Pap, Jane breaking in?'

'Sis, I can't even begin to even with this situation − it's officially wild. We need...'

A knock at the door. We didn't need that.

'Get that will you, one of you?' Pap shouted from behind a cupboard in the kitchen. Glasses clinked in the distance.

I shook my head. No. Not me. Norva stepped up to the door to answer it, looking through the peephole first.

She let out a loud short shriek. My heart raced. She slid slowly down the door, her hand on her mouth.

'Norva?' I said, the dull ache of dread even more acute. 'Who is it?'

She shook her head.

'Tell me!' I demanded.

She shook her head. 'See for yourself!'

I steeled myself, bracing myself for the worst. Cloud News? The police here to arrest Pap? A zombified Hugo? I shook that ridiculous thought away. I stepped over her, and leaned into the peephole.

Mark. Obviously. Her affection was utterly misdirected. Especially now.

'He's a suspect, Norva!' I whispered.

'I'm so confused,' she whimpered.

I shook my head at her, and she stood up. As I opened the door, Norva placed herself in the tight gap between it and the wall.

'Yes?' I asked him.

Mark stood there with his hands in his jeans pockets. 'Hi,' he said. He leaned close to me, peering into my face. I leaned away. 'Like, which one are you again? Neri or Norma?'

I could hear Norva's palpable dejection from behind the door. My sympathies for her were limited. That's what you get for 'loving' fools – and potential murderers. Little to no return on investment.

'Neither.'

'I'm here to see your Dad, innit.'

'Why?'

'I need to talk to him about something, about the madness happening around here.' He leaned on the doorframe.

Interesting.

'Suppose you should come in then,' I said.

Mark smiled brightly and stepped into the hall.

Norva screamed silently as he walked past.

We followed him to the kitchen, where he took a seat at the round table with Pap and Jane. The chair he dragged squeaked on the lino floor, leaving a raised welt. A little air bubble. Norva stared at it, hypnotised.

Even in the evening, the temperature settled at sweltering.

Jane mopped at her forehead with the bottom of her white t-shirt, while Pap welcomed Mark.

She thought no one was looking. She was wrong.

Mark sat down. All the chairs were taken, so we stood by the sink. I turned the cold tap on and off, running my hands underneath the intermittent stream.

Norva looked at me quizzically and muttered 'weird' under her breath.

It was calming. I needed to be calm. ' O h h , sandwiches!' Mark shouted, leaning over, hastily removing the cling film from the platter and grabbing two fistfuls.

'Help yourself,' I said sarcastically.

Norva shushed me. 'You're so welcome, Mark,' she said with a wide smile.

Another knock. Heart stop.

Pap asked me to get the door by throwing his head in its direction. I dug my nails into my palms during the short trip down the hall.

Through the peephole, I saw Serena, with a basketful of Vitonicas. Finally, something positive.

'Serena,' I began, opening the door. I didn't say more. I didn't have the words.

Her eyes filled with tears and she shrugged. 'I just didn't know where else to go, who to be with. I just met DCI Sharp and I need a moment.'

I welcomed her into the house, and walked her into the kitchen with my hand on her back. Norva gratefully took the basket and stocked the fridge with the juice.

The kitchen was silent. They didn't know what to say, either. Mark hung his head and fixed his gaze on the table. Pap stood up and offered Serena his seat, which she accepted. As she sat, he rubbed her shoulders and offered her a cheddar cheese sandwich on thin white bread. She inspected it, turning it over a few times in her hand. She took the smallest of bites and placed it on the table, wiping her mouth. She smiled, weakly. Jane turned away from her and sighed, irritated.

Another knock. Too many visitors. I was the butler now, so I went to answer it. I peered in the peephole: a duo with food.

Nina Shah. Mrs Kowlaski. Pakoras. Pierogis.

I let them in. Nina mumbled sympathetic words about the situation. She had seen the Cloud

News coverage. Mrs K smiled and walked in. She offered no words. In the kitchen, she threw her food in the centre of the table.

'Eat!' she demanded.

Mrs K stared at Mark for an uncomfortably long time. Catching on, he stood up and offered his seat.

The gang was all here. Our suspects drank tall glasses of juice with ice in silence.

Norva leaned against the fridge. 'So what happened at the meeting on Friday, everyone?'

19

'You don't already know this, girls? Your friend George was there,' Mrs Kowalski said with a smile, nodding at Nina.

'Yeah we heard,' Norva said. 'Nina, how was it? What happened?'

'Well, it was my first meeting, and probably my last...I'm a quiet person really. It was too much...'

Jane jumped in. 'Nina – I told you already – it's not normally like that, it was the annual fund-sharer. Everyone has different wants and needs,..' Her voice trailed away.

Nina turned to Pap. 'I totally got where you were coming from Joe, trust me, but The Hub was so hot, and the language you used. Hugo looked sick. It was too much of a roasting. In every sense.'

Serena started to sniff. 'I miss him so much.' She reached for her basket. 'I should go, I'm no use to anyone like this.'

Serena went to stand; Nina reached for her hand.

'Don't go,' she said gently. 'Stay with us, have some food. You're in good company.'

Was she? I looked over at Norva. She was looking at Mark.

Serena smiled weakly and sat back down. She bit into a pakora and smiled appreciatively at Nina, who held onto her other hand.

'I didn't know Hugo was sick?' I asked Serena, quietly.

'Yah,' she said, her eyes welling up. 'He had allergies all week, and was a tad dehydrated from the heat too, I think.'

'The heat?' laughed Mrs Kowalski. 'Just heat and not gin too?'

'What are you trying to say?' said Pap looking angrily at Mrs Kowalski.

My body stiffened.

'Nothing, nothing at all,' said Mrs Kowalski, popping a pierogi in her mouth. 'Why are you sticking up for Hugo anyway? You told him to watch himself!'

Norva and I looked at each other. Pap told Hugo to 'watch himself' too? Nothing good happened after Pap told you to 'watch yourself.'

'Everyone, please!' begged Serena, her head in her hands.

'Just a difference of opinion,' Jane offered, placing her hand on Pap's arm.

Visibly irritated by the conversation, he removed Jane's hand from his arm. It flopped conspicuously onto the table.

I shook thoughts of Hugo's arm away. Again.

'Mrs K, I just want the best for The Tri,' Pap said quietly. 'You – in particular – know this very well.'

What does she know in particular?

'You want the best? You do enough? Everything broken. Long list. Everything stink.' She wafted her hand in front of her face.

Mark reached over and took another fistful of food. One pakora, two pakora, three pakora, more.

'You know, speaking of stink – if people did their jobs, these girls wouldn't find bodies,' Mrs K added.

I took a sharp intake of breath. Norva whispered 'wow' under her breath.

'Enough! ENOUGH!' Serena screamed. She slammed her fists on the table.

Food flew into the air. Juice flowed across the table and Mark quickly cradled his plate.

'You are talking about my brother – my brother – as a body,' she shouted. 'We found him just today. Today! A few hours ago. Have you no compassion?'

Serena looked at Mrs K, who shrugged, and bit into a sandwich. She gagged, and spat it into her hand.

'Joe is our friend. Let DCI Sharp and her team do their work,' Serena continued, placing her hand on Pap's shoulder. 'I understood his reasoning at the meeting, and I stand by him.' She stood up, choking back her tears. 'Goodnight, everyone. Enjoy the Vitonicas.'

Serena paced down the hall, shutting the door quietly behind her. Those who were left at the table sat there in silence.

That was, until Mark awkwardly said 'well' and stood up from the table. He pocketed five sandwiches for his long journey home. An epic two doors down. Everyone else rose and shuffled out, keeping their eyes to the floor.

Norva held the door open. I'm certain she tried to sniff Mark's t-shirt as he left.

Pap leaned in the doorway outside his room. 'Girls, I'm done. I'll see you in the morning. If you need to talk, you know where I am.'

20

Norva shut our door and leaned against it. I immediately sat at our desk and shook the mouse, resuscitating the computer, opening our document. I looked at the to-dos.

'Sis,' she said in a low voice. 'What the actual flip was that? I don't even know where to begin.'

'We'll start here,' I said. 'Our first action was...'

I read it out to Norva.

To-do: Find out about the meeting

'Well, what do we actually know about it?' Norva wailed. 'Not that much!' She slid down the door and sat with her back against it. 'We know from Barry's star turn on the news that Pap and Hugo kicked off at the meeting and had a blazing row.'

I agreed. 'Yes, that's been corroborated by the suspects who were just here, in our kitchen. But I agree — we need more detail.'

Norva angled her hips to reach for her phone and then she sat back down. Stern-faced, she used both thumbs to spit out what looked like quite a demanding message.

'Texting George?' I asked.

'You're damn right I am,' she said, throwing her phone in front of her when her task was complete.

'Pap told Hugo to watch himself, Nik, he must have been really mad,' Norva said quietly.

'I know,' I replied. 'I'm actually frightened to find out the details.'

I looked back at the rest of our to-dos.

```
To-do: Find out where the suspects went after
the meeting
To-do: Ask Pap about his conversation and limp
To-do: Test The Hugo/Chute hypothesis
To-do: Ask Pap about the paint/bags
To-do: Close the time of death window
```

'Norva, we're not doing too well on the other items on our list either,' I said. 'We need to move quickly — Sharp will be all over this pretty quickly and…'

Norva crawled forward to grab her phone. 'Five minutes, George says. Then, we out.'

She looked over at me. 'And yeah, we have loads more things to find out, definitely. Urgently. A key one being, how the hell did Jane get into our flat? Because the door wasn't unlocked. As if!'

I span around in my chair.

'Right!?' I said. 'We would never.' I looked out of the window across the Tri and let out a small, bitter laugh. 'Any other time, that incident would have warranted an entire file for itself. Today, it's just a side mission of a bigger quest.'

Norva joined me at the window and used the telescope. Below us, the residents had gone home. May Burton and her ilk had packed their equipment away and begun to disperse. The Tri became yesterday's news, today.

Officer Burnett manned the cordon in Katie's place, the tape replaced.

'Do you think they'll have forgotten all about this in the morning?' I asked.

'Are you mad? No chance,' she snorted. 'The forensics haven't even arrived yet, by the looks of it. In five days, maybe? Sure. But not tomorrow. The media and Lady Sharp are gonna be all up in our business for a while yet.'

Ding! Ding!

'He's ready. Let's bounce.'

'Wait, wait! Keys? Bundles? Dog?' I asked.

'Oh yeah! You do the bundles; I'll get the keys.'

I nodded and began to prepare. 'The bundles' were the piles of clothes we stuffed in our beds if we were ever out when we shouldn't be. We had used them successfully two point five times to date.

The trouble was, a lot of the bundling went into the body this afternoon, which now lay in the refuse area. I took my quilt and put it under Norva's duvet. I scrunched it and shaped it so it looked like two of us were in the same bed.

Norva returned with the keys.

'Always in the kitchen!' she said, holding them near my face. She looked at her bed; her hand flew to her mouth. 'Nik, you put us together? On a day like today? It really fits the narrative, I swear. Beautiful, honestly. We'll be roasting, but bundle-me really needs bundle-you right now.'

Norva looked genuinely moved. For a split second.

'Alright, enough sap, let's move,' she said.

We crept past Pap's door and she held Ringo under her left arm, her right hand around his mouth. I opened the front door, triple-checking I had locked it. We quickly and lightly ran to the lift.

Norva pressed the button to take us to the lobby. 'I literally cannot believe George didn't tell us about this immediately. Some friend he is!' Norva whispered and hissed.

Hisspered.

I laughed internally at the new word I just created.

Norva continued, 'Said he's recorded the meeting, but couldn't send it over. Umbongoed it.'

'You mean embargoed it?'

'Hell does that mean anyway?'

'It means he didn't want to send it out yet. He was waiting to release it.'

'God, what is his problem?'

'He's just dedicated, I guess. You can't be mad with him Norva; he literally just saved us, and Pap.' Norva kissed her teeth. 'I can be mad with who I like, when I like to be honest.'

The lift stopped on the floor below.

I held my breath. I knew who it should be, but what if it wasn't?

The doors opened.

'Alright?' Norva said sullenly.

'How do, NSquared?' George whispered.

He stepped into the lift, holding his phone high in the air.

'What the...' Norva began, but George immediately shushed her.

'I'm sampling the sound for my new tune, 'Lift Up My Endz – open bracket – Corner Won – close bracket'. It's gonna be legit. Uploading it tonight. Watch me break the internet!'

We rode the lift in silence, while George sombrely felt at one with his soundscape.

I stifled laughs all the way down.

21

I turned on my phone's flashlight and shined it at George.

'I cannot wait to recreate this for you guys. I'm living!' He whispered, outside The Hub.

The doors were open, but no one was there.

'I thought Katie and her crew would be crawling all over this place, to be honest,' said George. 'Where they at? Where are those snowmen dusting for prints?'

'Too early for that, bro,' said Norva, stepping into the room. 'Plus, we heard they're super low on numbers, something happening up North. Just Katie, that Burnett guy and Scary Sharp. All eyes are on the scene. For now. We ahead of the game.' She tapped at her temple with her index finger.

'Yeah, you right!' said George. 'You smart, Norva.'

'I know this,' she replied.

I was over the compliments. 'Can we start please, George?'

'Aight, aight,' he said. He moved into the centre of the room. My torch tracked him.

'Context. It was 'Jane and the Tri-Angels dish-out-their-money night', yeah?'

'That's a hot band name, you know,' said Norva.

'I was sitting here.' He squatted on the spot. He ran to Barry's Burn. 'Jane was here.' Another squat. 'Your dad, Ole Joe was here.' He stepped left. A squat.

George ran to the middle of the room, coughed and hunched over. 'And Hugo was here.' He did a slow, feeble squat for effect.

Norva's eyes were bright as she followed him around the room. True friendship.

'It was absolutely roasting in here,' he continued, fanning his face. 'Some blonde kid was hanging out that window. The woman sitting here,' he pointed, 'had melted, basically. A puddle person.' He crumpled his body to the floor.

Norva roared with laughter and lay next to him. Impressive, yes, but not that funny. George was irritating. Norva was irritating. Together they were vexing.

'Please. George, Norva. Can we get to it? I understand you recorded the meeting, George?'

'Damn straight,' he said, reaching into his pockets for his phone. 'Glad I did too, because the internet is gonna LOVE this one – now I can share it.'

The video started. Slowly. It was mostly close-ups of George doing what he calls 'free styling'. I had Norva's support, for once.

'Scrub through it, George, god! Edit your content!'

Charity Jane sat at a table in front of Barry's Burn. Pap sat next to her. She spoke into the microphone. 'Yay, welcome to the 85th Tri-Angel meeting everyone!'

Screeching feedback.

Charity Jane leaned away from the microphone and applauded. 'Great to see so many new faces tonight. For those who don't know me, yet, I'm Jane Cooper, Chief Tri-Angel.'

George interjected, 'Yeah, she's a chief alright!'

Norva laughed. 'Innit, though.'

I shushed them.

'The Tri-Angels is a charity, run by and for me, I mean, us.' Jane laughed. 'It's for everyone on the estate. Together, we've raised thousands of pounds over the last five years to make improvements to our buildings and our lives! Thank you, all of you, for your continued support. Before we get into tonight, a couple of community notes for you.'

'Firstly, I'm so very proud and pleased to announce that Kwame Kent from Corner Two has been scouted by Crystal Palace Football Club! He will be officially joining the youth squad from September.'

The crowd erupted into applause and cheers. George turned the camera to his face, and stuck out his tongue. Behind him, Jane continued. 'Yes, excellent news! Don't forget us, Kwame! Secondly: a big angelic thank you to Serena from Corner One for providing the drinks tonight, Veronicas.'

'It's "Vitonica", Jane,' Serena shouted off-camera.

'That's the one! Thank you, Serena,' Jane said, tersely. 'It's great to see a Tri-business doing well. You could say its tri-mendous.'

The three of us groaned, along with the other people in the video.

George's video panned over to Serena who stood up, took a cheeky bow and waved to the group.

'Generous queen,' Norva remarked.

The video focused back on Jane.

'Now back to tonight – let's decide how we're going to spend the money we've raised over the last year. Five. Thousand. Pounds! Well done, all.'

George scrubbed through the video a bit more. 'Let's cut to the real. Where it gets *really* good.'

Hugo stood up, shakily. His skin was bright red. Heatstroke? Someone out of shot handed him a microphone.

'The Triangle Estate is a seminal example of Brutalist architecture.' There he goes. 'A style that's very much back in vogue, just in time for its 60th anniversary. The wider world, and the general public, are starting to understand just how brilliant and important these buildings are to us, our city and the world. The wider world and general public are starting to understand how well-made and beautiful they are.'

People laughed in the background. 'Well-made, my buttcheeks!' someone exclaimed. Others shushed him.

'We must give our thanks to the progressive vision of architect Ellis Silvertöe – for our homes, our community and our lives.'

A confused silence swept across The Hub.

'So what you saying, Hugo?' someone slurred at the back. Barry.

Hugo coughed nervously. He held onto his chest before speaking.

'What I'm saying is, I think we should use the money to erect a statue to commemorate the anniversary of The Tri. Celebrate the work Ellis Silvertöe and by extension other great architects and artists of the period, you know, Clockenstien – I adore Clockenstien – De Bouseier, Sir Pence, et cetera.'

Hugo slumped in his chair. Serena reached into a cool bag and handed him a juice. He leant on her appreciatively as he drank. He was immediately cooler and calmer.

The calm didn't extend to the rest of the room, though. George's camera spun around.

Someone at the back shouted, 'Hugo. Hugo. Hugo! Put on your knickers before your coat, nameen? It's a heatwave, bro. We out here suffocating, we need aircon – and you're talking about a statue!? I'm perplexed!'

A voice at the front. 'Hugo, you're being an utter pleb, to be honest. We need better lifts, renovations, a new health centre, a nursery, double-glazing to sort out the noise. That's just for starters.'

People cheered.

I spotted Mrs Kowalski nodding her head with closed eyes at this suggestion.

Someone off camera – George really needed to work on his camera skills – said: 'You know what, though? A statue might be alright. Something positive and impactful. Five thousand isn't going to scratch the surface of the work that needs doing. We need millions for that. So, why not get something, you know, that's just *nice* for once?'

The crowd murmured at the possibility. George panned over them. There was Mark. Mouth agape. Eyes narrowed. Norva squealed.

Pap stood up and walked around the table. With ease.

'No limp!' I whispered.

22

'Hugo.' Pap perched at the edge of the table. 'How is that a good suggestion? Don't you want more room for the work you do here?' His voice got louder. 'Wouldn't that be better than a statue?' He shouted, 'Or a plaque!?' He threw down his papers.

Jane tugged at Pap's arm to calm him. It worked.

Mrs K stood up. She reminisced. 'You know – this place was wonderful when it open. Beautiful.' People in the group murmured in agreement. 'I remember I came here with Mr K. We didn't live here then – was a dream. We went to the chip shop, and then Third Avenue to look over and throw chips at the tiny ant people below. And now, The Tri is falling apart…'

Pap jumped in. 'See! See! Thank you Mrs K! I knew you would understand.' He turned to look at Hugo. 'And you want a statue?'

'I'm not finished!' Mrs K continued sternly. 'So I think something that brings back the love and glamour would be great. I like the statue. It's positive.'

Pap looked confused and exasperated. Mrs K laughed to herself.

Barry stood up. 'I hear you, Joe. Bermuda's could do with some work. We get it all on this estate. Noise, pollution, burnt-out cars, people peeing in the stairwells. We need more cameras,' Pap nodded vigorously. 'But five grand is not going to fix that. Plus, the council should be doing that anyway!'

Hugo nodded vigorously.

Pap caught his eye. His anger rose.

'Alright, Hugo Two-surnames. Since you're apparently so rich, pay for it yourself!'

The crowd gasped.

Hugo replied slowly, 'Look, I don't know why you think I've got money – don't let my name fool you, Joe. I just think it's important that we celebrate people and places where we can. With the Tri's imminent anniversary, we should celebrate her, all her corners; her beauty, the best times, the tumultuous times. Let's, erm, 'shout out' Silvertöe.'

He coughed loudly. Serena leaned into him. He continued. 'We get a statue, lovingly crafted by someone like Lavenderstick or Clockenstein. It will draw people from outside the estate; they will take note of the conditions – and the community spirit – and we'll unlock more money. It's like my antiques. You have to spend money to make money. So, let's keep on trying for The Tri.'

The crowd murmured their approval.

'You're bloody trying, Hugo – trying my patience.' Pap slammed his fist on the table.

I looked away from the video and over at Norva who had pursed her lips and shut her eyes. She shook her head to dismiss what she was hearing.

Pap looked angry.

Really angry.

'OK, everyone! I think we've heard all sides,' said Charity Jane, nervously, trying to break the tension. 'Let's get this one to a vote. Exciting!'

'We have two options. Those in favour of investing in Joseph's upkeep plan, raise your hands.'

The camera whipped around the room. Approximately 43% of people had their hand up.

'Now, those who support Hugo's Silvertöe statue, raise your hands.' Jane looked nervous.

George made an awkward face to camera. He whipped his phone around the room. 51% of hands. I couldn't account for the other 6%. It was close, certainly, but not that close. Hugo had it.

The Hub was uncomfortably silent. Someone at the back cut through it.

'He has a point, Joseph. There's not enough money at play to make a difference, so let's take a punt on this. This is his world – he gets this stuff.'

Pap exploded. 'So what – that's it? I'm not a good enough caretaker for you now? Why don't you just let Hugo run this place. Yeah, that's a good plan, let him do it. I've been here for 25 years, I grew up here. Tri through and through! I did my best for you – all of you. This guy only moved here for jokes. For fun. *For the experience.* Oh, you didn't know that!? Well you do now. Our lives are a tourist attraction for him! A human zoo! This is your king?' he spat at the room.

George loved that last line, and mimicked it perfectly.

Pap was foaming at the mouth.

The camera moved back to Hugo. He looked weak and shivered in his seat.

'Hugo looks mash up, right?' said George. 'I reckon he was on his special water, sozzled probs.'

'It looks like heat stroke to me,' I said.

I looked at the other people in the room. Everyone who could look red, looked very red indeed. Everyone fanned themselves in the heat.

'Joseph, yes, you know I was inspired to move here for the architecture,' Hugo started cautiously. 'But I absolutely love it here – I'm a true resident, I contribute…'

Pap snorted. 'Oh, you contribute do you?' He shot a look at Jane, who started to interject but decided to look silently at the floor.

'I love the community,' Hugo continued. 'I want the best for it – I'm just trying to think long-term here.'

Pap was furious. 'So I'm short-sighted now? I'm a blind man? Well I see you Hugo! I see you clearly! You've all gone mad! Hugo – you better watch yourself, mate. I mean that. So help me – stay out of my way.'

23

Pap slammed his fist on the table, and stormed out of The Hub. Charity Jane looked around the room and quickly followed him.

The video moved over to Serena and Hugo talking to Mrs K.

'Absolute madness,' said George to the camera, before sticking his tongue out.

The video ended abruptly.

I felt sick.

Pap was implicated. Without a doubt. The motive seemed clear. My hands shook. I looked over at Norva in the dark. She was chewing at the end of her braid. Nerves.

'What time did the meeting end, George?' I asked.

'Ten-thirty ish?'

I double-checked our notes. Corroborated.

'George, where did you go after the meeting?'

Time to rule out some suspects.

George looked at the floor. 'OK, you need to swear you won't tell my mum about this, yeah?'

'Yes,' I said confidently.

Norva narrowed her eyes. 'What did you do?' she asked suspiciously.

'So listen, yeah, don't be mad Norv, but I blagged my way into TrojKat's gig and I flipping went backstage. Backstage! She remembered me from back in the day. Gave her my SoundCloud – of course – and she's gonna check it out. Said she's thinking about coming back to The Tri to do her next video. Oh my god, it was beyond lit, girl! It was a raging inferno.'

Norva's mouth fell open. 'You went to see TrojKat. Without me. You went backstage. And you didn't tell me. Have I got that right?'

'I took my chance, Norva, I just had to do it,' George pleaded. 'Don't hate. It was a once in a lifetime flex.'

TrojKat, also known as Katarzyna Clarke, was a singer who used to live in Corner Two. Norva often told me that 'TrojKat was blowing up right now', which I assumed meant she was popular. Popular with Norva and George anyway.

Norva shook with rage. 'You're dead to me, George, deader than Hugo.'

George and I leaned away from Norva, shocked.

'Girl, that's way too strong,' he said.

'Yeah, well, strong is bailing on me and keeping this quiet,' she said. 'Anyway, you might be lying, where's the receipts?'

George pulled out his phone. 'I have a till roll of them, sis.'

He flicked through his photos. 'Look, here I am outside the GoTo.' A selfie outside the venue.

'Here's me inside.' George sticking out his tongue next to the bar.

'There's our girl, killing it on stage.' A blurred shot of TrojKat.

'Here's me chilling out back with the legend herself.' A close up of George and TrojKat hugging.

Norva snatched George's phone. 'Let me see! She zoomed into the photos, checked the times and the locations.

'He's telling the truth – he was there. He is a traitor.' She tossed his phone back at him – he caught it. Just.

'Easy, Norv, I don't have the coins for insurance.'

'But George, how long were you there. Where was your mum?' I asked.

'Ah yeah, that bit's not so fire,' he said. 'My aunt, Geeta, is going through it with her man right now. Real dark times. Friday night, she gets home, he's just up and bounced. No trace.'

'For real?' said Norva, sympathy seeping back. 'I knew it was bad, but not that bad.'

'Yeah,' said George, 'after the meeting, Mum went over to stay the night. I was going too. I walked Mum to the Tube, saw the poster for the gig and was like, you know what this is my moment.'

'So much for 'family first,'' snorted Norva.

'What did you do?' I asked, moving the conversation along.

'Well, I'm not proud of this,' sighed George, 'but I said "Ma, I left my mic back at The Tri, let me catch you up".'

Norva shook her head, 'You shouldn't lie to Nina, she's too pure.'

'Yeah I know, I don't feel good about it,' said George. 'Anyway, after the gig, I headed there. They were drinking wine and weeping, didn't notice me. Next morning, we came home, like lunchtime.'

He swiped through his phone.

'Here look, here a pic of all of us the next day.' He pushed the phone in our faces. 'Call Aunty G if you want, but don't ask her the details – she's keeping her ghosting on the down low.'

'OK, the Khans are officially ruled out,' sighed Norva. She looked at me, and I nodded in the affirmative.

George laughed. 'LOOOL.'

He actually said 'lol'.

'As if The Khans were really in the mix!? You're too much, NSquared, but I'll allow. I only murder bass and merc the internet.'

'We have to be thorough,' I said, quietly.

Norva laughed. 'I'm still mad with you, though.'

'Never that,' said George. 'Next time, you can be my plus one.' He punched her playfully on her arm.

I rolled my eyes.

Taking the hint, possibly, George said, 'Listen, sisters, I have to bounce. My midnight adventures have drawn to a close. Today has been a ride, thanks to you. I need to finish up my tune in the morning, so I need to be fresh and on point for the lyrics to flow. Come up and see Serena tomorrow and knock for me after − although I'll probably hear you. Those walls are thin. I heard her crying earlier.'

I shook my head. 'Poor Serena, it's awful for *me*, let alone for *her.* His sister.'

'Totally,' said George, 'and in other Serena-related news, we have some of that Vitonica in the fridge, Nik. I hear it's your jam. Baby needs her bottle waaaaah!' George said, and wailed like a baby. He shook his fist near his eyes.

Norva stifled a laugh and looked at the floor. I made a face and stuck out my tongue.

I regretted that instantly. Not my style.

24

We walked in circles around The Hub once George left. I shone my phone's torch around the walls. Hugo's desk caught the light.

'He didn't die in here,' Norva said. 'Too clean, too tidy and as I said, the cops aren't sniffing around yet, so nope. Supports my "died in murderer's flat theory". You'll see I'm right.'

I ran my fingers across Hugo's desk, while Norva sat in his chair. She did an impression of him. 'We all wear masks in public, metaphorically speaking. It's seminal.'

It was spot on. I had to laugh. I knelt down beside her. A drawer. I pulled at it two times, but it was locked.

Norva pushed the chair away from the desk.

'My department. Move.' She yanked at the drawer.
Hard.

It moved the desk, but the drawer remaimed
locked.

Attempt two. Same result.

'Can't believe that didn't work,' Norva said,
sitting back on her knees. 'This might though.' She stuck
her hands in her pockets, pulling them outside of dress.

Now on the floor:
- dusty crumbs from stale biscuits
- three chocolate wrappers
- a crumpled tissue

Norva knelt down to look through the debris.
'Ah, there it is.'

- a small black hair pin

'Norva,' I could feel my eyes rolling, 'that's not a
thing that works in real life.'

'No smoke without fire,' she said.

'That doesn't even make sense,' I said, confused.

'Shuussh, just direct the light!'

Norva stuck the pin in the lock. Twisted it slowly

left, twisted it slowly right. Nothing. Seemingly defeated, she twisted it back left and right vigorously.

There was a satisfying clunk as the lock released itself. We looked at each other, amazed.

'Yo, I cannot believe that actually worked...' she whispered to herself, looking down at her hands, turning them over. 'My gosh, I guess I was an Avenger this whole time, and now I'm just finding my powers!' She laughed.

The drawer was a mess, surprisingly. I assumed Hugo was neat.

- Two unopened letters – HMRC
- 17 receipts
- One lip balm – Lychee Lemonade
- 12 half chewed pens
- Three folded newspapers (one dated December 1981)
- Five fast food wrappers
- Eight dirty, but dry, paint brushes
- One signed photo of someone called David Dickinson, whoever that was

I reached to the back of the drawer. Underneath a fraying mouse mat was a small trinket. A stone-coloured, pyramid-shaped ornament, with many multi-coloured scratches etched on it. Five centimetres square. I shone my light at my hand. It fitted perfectly in my palm.

'What's that then?' asked Norva, peering into my hand.

'Ah, one of Hugo's bits of junk, I think,' I replied.

It wasn't a bit of junk. I knew what it was. It was the lid to one Hugo's vases. A tall, slim vase in the same stone, with the same coloured scratches.

It was always on his desk. I asked him about it once. 'It's rare, darling Anika. A vase with a lid, in this style? Absolutely unique. Seminal,' he said, running his many-ringed fingers around it.

'This is dry. I'm checking out the rest of this place,' said Norva, turning on her own light, skipping off.

I ran my fingers over the lid. Instant comfort. I looked up over the desk and saw Norva poking around in a waste bin. That's when I decided to break a rule. Keeping my eyes on Norva, I stuffed the lid in the right pocket of my shorts. And stole it.

It was official – another criminal was at large on The Tri.

I stood up and felt my new unlucky charm in my pocket. It felt uncomfortably good and brought back memories of better times.

No regrets.

'Time to bounce, I reckon,' said Norva from across the room, breaking my thoughts.

I joined her to peruse the bin.

- Three empty bottles of Vitonica
- Five fermenting pierogis
- Two chocolate wrappers
- Ants everywhere
- Flies: five dead, three alive

Positively hygienic, compared to the bin she looked through earlier today.

'Yes, we're done here,' I agreed. 'We know the meeting was about money.'

Motive: Money?

'Yeah, and how to spend it,' Norva said. 'I'm firmly on Team Pap. Repairs for the win.'

'Hugo had a point, though,' I said. 'Good will and publicity could attract even more money.'

She shot me a confused, angry look. 'Whose side you're on, Sis?'

'I don't think it's a good idea to talk about 'sides', when referring to Pap and Hugo, Norva, not today.'

'Yeah, you're 'right,' she said.

To-do: Find out about the meeting

We walked to the lobby. I yawned.

'Yeah, I'm knackered too,' Norva said. Right. The plan is this. Bed. Brief sleep. Tomorrow – the market, talk to suspects, hunt motives.' She leaned against the lift.

To-do: Whitford Market

'You know who looks like they have a motive?' I began. 'A really big one?'

'Don't say it,' Norva said quietly. 'I know.'

'He's the clear suspect, Norva – and I'm terrified! We need to get to him before DCI Sharp does. We need to know where he was, and how he got that limp…'

'But, you know he didn't do it, right?' Norva said, jumping in. 'Where's your family values? Your loyalty?'

'It's not about loyalty, Norva,' I said quietly. 'It's about how it looks. And right now, it looks really bad.'

25

We gently put the key into the front door, and closed it silently behind us.

'…and the girls, my daughters — Anika and Norva — you may have seen them…'

'I have indeed,' replied DCI Sharp.

I gasped. A breath caught in my throat. Norva grabbed my hand and we pushed ourselves against the wall outside our room.

'…they came running in, 'Hugo's in the bin! Hugo's in the bin!'' Pap choked up. 'Nik really liked him.' His voice broke. 'For her to see him like that, it breaks my heart. It hurts, you know?'

'I understand,' she said. 'You want the very best for them.'

'If I can't even protect them where they live,

how can I protect them out in the world?' He sniffed. Momentary silence. 'So, yeah, sorry about that.' He coughed. 'That's pretty much it. I hope that helps.'

'Very much,' she said. 'If there's anything else you remember, here's my card. Just let me know. Anything, anything at all.'

'Will do.'

'Thanks for all your help today, and for use of your office. It's just a temporary measure.'

'Sure, sure.'

DCI Sharp stood up to leave. We quickly darted into our room. Pap walked her to the door and went to bed.

Hugo_down_2307.doc

Victim: Hugo Knightley-Webb
Body location: Corner One Refuse Area
Date and Time of discovery: 23/07 14:27

Time of death: Between Fri 20/07 22:30 and
Sat 06:30
Weapon: Paint can

Motive: Money?

Hypothesis: Murdered in Corner One flat, either
floor 21 or 22, with paint can, placed in chute

To-do: Find out about the meeting
To-do: Find out where the suspects went after
the meeting
To-do: Ask Pap about his conversation and
limp
To-do: Test The Hugo/Chute hypothesis
To-do: Ask Pap about the paint/bags
To-do: Close the time of death window
To-do: Go to Whitford Market

	221 Pap ~~Nik~~ ~~Noeva~~ ~~Ringe~~	222 Mrs Kowalski	223 Mark Walker ~~'Mother'~~	211 ~~George Shah~~ ~~Nina Shah~~	212 ~~Hugo KW~~ Serena KW	213 Charity Jane
Suspect's alibi during TOD window	Out until 01:27	Working on a project with 'a friend'.		GS: Backstage with TrojKat NS: With Aunt Geeta		
Corroborated?						
Motivation?	Argument at Friday's meeting over money.			Y – photographic evidence for both suspects.		
Questions?						How did you get into our flat?

138

26

I woke up at 06:32 and headed straight to Pap's room. His door was open, but he was gone. Bed made, curtains open. I reached for my phone. My heart beat fast.

Where are you?

Had Pap been arrested? Did DCI Sharp come back for him? I returned to our room and sat nervously on my bed. Norva and Ringo snored gently, in unison, on top of her quilt. I looked out of the window onto the Tri.

Two police cars below. It began. Again.

Ding! Ding!

Morning, luv! I left a note in the kitchen. 1st aid training + meeting at council + painting later :(Be back 2nite. B gud! x

I was relieved, but my heart still sank. I needed to speak to him. Urgently.

Ding! Ding!

P.S. Katie and Police using office as their base.

Yes, Pap. I know. Way ahead of you.

'Norva, wake up,' I said gently, sitting at the end of her bed. Ringo raised an ear and looked at me with one eye. Norva murmured in her sleep. 'You're so strange, Mark,' she giggled.

Gross.

'Norva!' I shouted.

She woke up with a start. 'What! What's happening?' she shouted. She slowly opened her eyes and fixed them on me.

'Why you do that for?' she said sleepily. 'It was just getting good! I feel robbed.'

'Norva, we need to get going. Pap's out for the day, the police are in his office – let's go.'

'Alright, alright, ALRIGHT!' she shouted, sitting up and rubbing her eyes.

Ringo jumped off the bed and Norva dusted dog hair from her arms.

'Let me grab a quick shower.'

* * *

'I set up alerts for Hugo and The Tri across social platforms,' I said, sipping on a Vitonica. 'Want to look through them before we go?'

'Yas, sis!' she said surprised. 'You smart. Let's do it. What you got?' She sat down next to me at the kitchen table.

I opened Twitter and scrolled through.

'This one's from loKKKal_hero,' I read aloud.

ANOTHER incident on that mistake estate. About time they knocked it down that eyesore and moved those undesirables OUT of London.

Norva shook her head. 'Oh, so we're rodents now? That's lovely.'

There was another from LDNpoet:

Trying times
On The Tri
What could be the angle?
A-cute death of an
Obtuse tenant?

Comedians everywhere, yet none were funny. I linked their 'commentary' into our files.

And opened YouTube. Three videos:

A short vlog from a 'ClaireCrocker' who claimed she lived on Corner Four.

'Corner Four!' Norva snorted.

'There aren't four corners in a triangle. Try harder, you vulture!'

Claire offered sympathy for Serena. She wailed into the camera. 'Leave The Tri Alone!' she screamed from under a bed sheet. Suddenly, cheering up, she said, 'Smash Subscribe and give the Like button a big thumbs up. Turn on those notifications, so you never miss a video!'

The second was a portrait-shot phone footage of the crowd around the refuse area yesterday afternoon.

'Ooh there's us! Fame!' Norva shouted as the camera quickly panned past us. We stood to the side, talking.

'I'm going to slow this down,' I said, clicking the cog, reducing the speed to 0.25. Let me see if we can spot any of the suspects.'

Norva looked at me in awe.

'Don't be impressed, Norva, this is basic stuff.'

The video slowed.

'There's Mrs K,' said Norva. She passed with her pierogies, offering one to the camera.

Jane and Pap stood at the front. Jane dabbed at her eyes with the heel of her hand. The camera moved slowly towards the lobby, behind us.

'Oh my days,' said Norva. 'What's going on there?'.

I squinted at the screen.

Serena and Mark talked quietly. They stood close together. Deep in conversation.

'What *is* this?' said Norva.

Mark talks, Serena nods. She opens her mouth to speak as Barry approaches. Barry puts his hand on Serena's shoulder. She turns away from Mark and begins to wail. She runs past us towards Pap and Jane, screaming. Mark's eyes follow her.

We look at each other. 'He was also in her flat, just before this,' I added.

Norva's eyes narrowed.

```
To-do: Find out what were Mark and Serena
talking about 23/07 c15:11
```

The final YouTube Video was May Burton's Cloud News report. My heart sank. Maybe the channel would cut Barry out?

No, of course not. It was ratings gold. There was Barry's accusation. There we were, standing next to a shocked Pap. There we went, pacing back to the lobby. I scanned the comments. They weren't disabled.

'The black man did it!' sat at the top.

I gulped and scrolled back to the video.

We weren't the only people caught on camera. Mrs Kowalski made a spectacle of herself, in her spectacles.

'Good riddance to bad rubbish,' she said, staring down the camera.

'I'll be back at The Tri to follow this up,' said May, wrapping up her report. 'Tomorrow,' she vowed.

Norva laughed nervously, 'Kowalski's got more ham than a pig.'

Her smiled dimmed. 'I'm still scared of her though. Her theatrical ways have me shook.'

'Same,' I replied.

27

The lift made its way up to us from the ground floor. Norva cradled Ringo in her arms. He licked at her face and mouth.

'I love you, fur baby,' she sung to him.

Repeatedly. Lullaby-style. It wasn't annoying. Not at all.

The lift creaked opened. Mrs K appeared between the doors. Norva dropped Ringo. He landed on his feet and shook himself down. Stray white hairs flew everywhere and I held my breath.

'Girls,' she said. 'How are you?'

'Fine,' I replied shortly.

Ringo trotted into the lift and sat down.

'We just saw you on the internet!' Norva said.

Mrs K's face brightened. 'Oh yes? Send me the link?'

'Yep,' said Norva.

Mrs K stepped out of the lift.

Seven bags wrapped around her right arm today. Up two from yesterday. Going for a record, I suppose.

'Still too hot in there.'

'Roasting,' said Norva. 'Mrs K, how's your project? Did you finish it?'

She looked at us.

'Yes, I did.' She smiled, weakly. 'Saturday morning about one fifteen. I'm very happy with the results. My friend was a great help.'

I shivered.

'He?' Norva asked.

'Yes,' she laughed. 'You know him, but I like my secrets.'

'Why though?'

'Ah, I don't want trouble.'

'What's the project?' I asked, trying to sound natural. Trying to sound bright and positive.

'A big clean up.'

'Why did you work so late, Mrs K?' said Norva. 'Everyone needs at least eight good hours of sleep. Keeps you beautiful.'

'I am beautiful!' she shouted. 'And, I had, what you could call, a deadline.' She laughed.

'Then, I slept like a baby. My work was done. I was at peace.'

I could feel Norva's eyes on me.

'Can we see your project? I bet it's beautiful!' I said.

'Well there's not much to see, not now,' she said. The lift doors closed on her smiling face.

'Who the hell is 'he', what's the project, and why is she at peace now?' said Norva.

In the lift down, I added notes to our table.

28

We passed the Murder Investigation Room, formerly Pap's office, on our way out. The door was ajar, and we craned our necks inside to have a look.

Officer Burnett sat at Pap's desk, but not at Pap's computer. He had pushed that relic to the edge, and sat typing away at a laptop. He didn't look up. Above him, on the opposite wall, was a floorplan of Corner One. Floors 21 and 22 were circled in thick red marker.

Next to that, a photo of Hugo, taken when he was alive. Next to that, a photo of Hugo's arm and hand, taken once he was dead.

I shuddered. Immediate flashback. Instant stomach ache.

'Once he's back, we'll bring him in for questioning,' said DCI Sharp, talking into her mobile from the other side of the office.

Panic. Who? Pap?

I stared at Norva. She fluttered her hand at me to dismiss my reaction. But I saw her gulp.

'And get me some more Officers!' she barked. 'This is ridiculous!'

DCI Sharp walked past the gap in the door, her phone to her face. We jumped back, gasping, but – too late. She turned and spotted us in the frame. Without reacting, she shut the door silently, while looking in our eyes.

We left the lobby.

'You know what,' said Norva. 'If this wasn't officially The Worst Time, I would totally ask Lady Sharp to be my mentor. She serves icy realness, and I kind of love it.'

***

The quickest, most direct route to the market from The Tri is via The Rec, through Corners two and three. We crossed it, walking straight through a basketball game.

'Time ain't on our side, sis!' Norva said, stomping.

'Keep it moving.'

I crept apologetically behind her, mouthing 'sorry' silently to the group.

'Oi, get off the court, wastegirls!' the team shouted.

The basketball flew, intentionally, at Norva's head. She swung round and dipped her body, contorting her torso. The ball narrowly missed her face.

'Nice try, LeBrons,' she laughed at them.

Ringo jerked on his lead. Before Norva could stop him, he lifted a whole chicken bone into his mouth. When she tried to retrieve it from his jaw, he showed his true nature.

His satanic hound form.

Ringo turned his head slowly and snarled. He bared his teeth and snapped at her fingers.

Norva was unperturbed. 'But baby, you'll slice up your throat,' she whimpered at him. 'And then what?'

Like he understood. Or cared.

While Norva tended to her child, I glanced back at Corner One. Perfect timing. Katie was striding across The Tri, back to the Investigation Room, I presumed.

'Katie! Katie!' Norva shouted. 'How goes it? 'Yesterday seemed super tough.'

Katie slowed down to speak to us. 'Yeah it was, and to be honest, girls – you're not helping.'

Norva pretended to look crestfallen.

Katie noticed. 'I'm sorry, Norv, but I really do need to concentrate. I've got loads on today – house-to-house interviews, more community liaison. I've barely had enough sleep. We're incredibly short on Officers – it's just ridiculous. I'm so tired.'

'What time did you leave last night?' I asked.

'This morning, you mean,' said Katie. 'About four. Once the forensics were complete, and the coroner finally showed up.' She yawned.

If it wasn't for effect, the timing was perfect.

'So late,' she continued. 'I could barely lift anything, some of the evidence was so heavy.'

'Like the paint can…' I asked.

'Yeah the murder weapon,' added Norva, her eyes shining.

'Murder weapon? Wait, what? How do you know about the paint can?' Kate said, surprised. 'I never told you anything about that?'

Norva looked at me. 'We found him, remember,' she said to Katie, rolling her eyes.

'Ah, OK! Of course. Sorry, I forgot that for a moment,' Katie said, giving me a weak smile.

'So the paint can is the murder weapon, right?' Norva probed.

'Girls, please,' she said. 'I can't…'

Katie began to walk away. She refused to meet our eyes. She was serious.

'Katie!' Norva called out to her.

She kept walking. Her pace increased.

'Katie, please stop. Just for a second,' Norva pleaded.

She stopped reluctantly. Norva touched her shoulder gently.

'Look, we get it. We know you can't chat police business. We know you're official, proper, legit. We know. We're proud. But come on, sis, throw us a bone on the paint can! If it's the murder weapon, blink twice for yes, Katie. That's all you have to do. Then we'll leave you alone.'

Katie sighed. She blinked twice, slowly.

'I really can't talk about this, girls,' she said gently, looking at us with sad eyes before turning her head. She walked away without looking back.

Weapon: Paint can - most likely. Suggested by Katie: 24/07 09:02

I looked at Norva. 'Confirmation on the paint can received.' I sighed. 'I've only ever seen them locked up in Pap's office. Or with Pap and Mark.'

'So?' said Norva.

'So,' I started slowly. 'This, again, really focuses the investigation on Pap – and now Mark, doesn't it.'

Norva shrugged her shoulders. 'Hmmm, does it, though?'

I looked at her incredulously. She couldn't be serious. 'Norva, don't let loyalty…'

'Come on, Nik,' she snapped. 'Look where we are. This is The Tri. You can get *anything* here if you really wanted it. Anything. Be 100% less naive.' She continued. 'All we know is it's blunt force trauma – also known as a massive blow to the nut. It could be any of them – Kowalski is strong as hell too. Look at all the bags she carries!'

My stomach burned in violent undisclosed disagreement.

'Let's get to the market,' Norva said, breaking the silence. 'It's not back until Sunday, right?'

I nodded.

'We'll miss our chance to chat to the traders if we don't get there sharpish.'

Good point.

We went via Better Buy. Norva 'needed' a patty for the journey, and I could always do with a juice.

Another scorching hot morning. 25 degrees already with no sign of stopping. I was thirsty.

We tied Ringo in the shade, and he quickly fell asleep, with a sigh.

Sissy wheeled herself out from behind her till, away from her fan. Sweat sprung from her forehead immediately.

'Hello sisters!'

We nodded a lethargic hello at her.

'God bless you both today,' She looked down. 'Especially today.'

Norva's eyes narrowed immediately. 'What do you mean, "especially today" Sissy?'

'Well, you know. People are talking – a whole lot of chatter. I don't think your dad, you know, did it. But that's the talk. Especially from Corner Threes. They're mad that they're way down on the repair list, but God bless. Their turn is coming!' Sissy smiled at us.

That smile quickly faded as Norva exploded.

'Why would you say that Sissy!? Why you out here telling us you think our dad is a murderer? You should be ashamed,' she spat. 'He got you this job, didn't he? God needs to bless *you*!'

Sissy was, as Norva would say, 'shook'. Her embarrassment was palpable.

'I'm just saying…' she said quietly to the floor. Her voice trailed away.

'Well don't *just say*. Speak less. Especially to us.'

Norva turned on her heel and stomped to the back of the shop.

I shook my head at Sissy, and ran up the aisle to join her.

We put our faces through the plastic strips that covered the large fridge. Temporary relief from the heat. And the rage.

Norva's eyes were full of tears. She angrily snatched and opened a bottle of water. I reached for a Vitonica. £1.50 in here. No thanks. Too expensive.

I held it in my hands, though.

'I thought you loved gossip,' I whispered lightly, trying to calm her.

'Truth,' she said, a tear rolling down her face. 'But not gossip about us. About our family. Our family being murderers? Nah. There's a line – and it just got long-jumped by Hot Wheels over there.'

Norva kissed her teeth. She guzzled and glugged down the full bottle of water in one go and put the empty crumpled bottle back on the shelf.

'Ain't paying for that!' she shouted. 'And she can stuff her patty where the sun don't shine.'

29

Whitford Market was very nice.

That was official, not just opinion. Five out of Five, according to *Time Out.*

It may just be one point eight miles west of The Tri, but it was worlds apart. Fancy. The refined face of London. It was in a film once, too, apparently. I've never seen it, though.

Whitford Market was heaving today. People were buying, selling, smelling, tasting. Curries, cheeses, cash. Stallholders were shouting, selling and smiling.

No rain to stop play. A good day. For everyone. Especially the tourists, who spoke loudly in a number of languages to each other.

Welcome to London.

'Wish I'd got a patty now, I'm well hungry,' moaned Norva, as we pushed our way through the crowds. 'Regrets.'

I pointed to a deli on a corner. She shrugged in agreement and we stumbled over.

We peered through the window.

The customers inside happily sipped coffees with extravagant, unpronounceable names.

'What!' Norva exclaimed. 'That sandwich there is £8.00! For cheese and bread? What is this life?'

I shrugged. 'City life. Let's get to the stall and go home. There's food in the fridge.'

I sounded like Pap.

Norva whined, 'But I'm hungry now!'

We walked on. I knew exactly where to find Hugo's stall. Art Club went there once. Last summer's field trip.

Hugo talked about his stall all the time. He also talked a lot about Timothy, The Fabric Man – the person who had recently acquired the stall next to his.

'Fabulous chap,' Hugo would say, 'with fabulous fabrics. Opulent and sumptuous.'

He would then chuckle quietly to himself.

The heaving crowd carried us to Hugo's pitch.

A table stood in its place. On top of it, a black and white photograph of Hugo smiled at us. His curly white hair bounced out of the frame. His hand, with its many rings on his fingers, touched his face.

I bit my bottom lip. No tears. Not now.

'What kind of 1980s, faded-in-the-window, forgotten, budget-hairdresser picture is that supposed to be?' said Norva. 'Do the man some justice!'

'Norva, please!' I said. 'I think it's nice.'

She snorted.

A large wreath of flowers lay next to the frame.

The card attached said: 'The Whitford Family love you, Hugo.'

An unstoppable tear rolled down my face.

The fabric stall stood to the right of Hugo's pitch. Silk, satin, suede. Gold, silver, bronze.

The stall was surrounded by customers who ran their hands over the wares. They murmured in appreciation.

'It's just cloth. Dial it back, jeez,' said Norva.

We waited until the crowd dispersed a little before we approached.

'Excuse me, sir?' I asked.

Norva rolled her eyes at 'sir'.

The man looked us up and down and stood tall.

'Yeah?' he replied in an American accent.

'You're Timothy, The Fabric Man, right?'

'Sure am, who's asking?'

'We're friends of Hugo's,' I said, pointing to his stall.

His body relaxed.

'Oh man,' he said. 'It's so heavy, man.'

He shook his head. He squinted at me. 'Oh wait, I remember you! Hugo's favourite student.'

I beamed. I knew it! 'You used to have hair, right? What happened?'

30

Timothy, The Fabric Man, early 40's I suppose. Long brown-grey hair, green eyes, beard.

'The Whitford Family are truly bummed out by the news, man.' He ran his hands through his hair. 'He was a righteous dude.'

'Yes. He was,' I agreed. It felt awful – and wrong – talking about Hugo in the past tense.

He was really gone. I felt a wave of pain in my stomach. I held back tears by biting my lip.

Norva noticed and touched my arm.

'Have you spoken to the Police yet?' I said, looking at the floor.

I looked up to see him shaking his head.

'Did you see him on Saturday? Did he come to

work?' asked Norva.

'Nah, he didn't pitch up. I was surprised, man. No, wait, actually, not *that* surprised. He was feeling really grody on Tuesday.'

'Grody?' Norva asked, confused.

'Like totally sick, but not good sick, like totally ill. Said he had loads of ants in his house. Dead and alive. He was coughing and red. Thought that's how he went – not murder. Who'd kill Hugo?' he shook his head.

I made a note. Ants. Redness. He was red in the video of the meeting. Not heatstroke?

'That's what we want to know,' said Norva.

'Oh really? That's rad, you're on it. I'm impressed.'

'Thanks, man!' Norva replied, pleased that someone was taking our work seriously.

'Do you mind if we ask you some questions?' I asked.

'Go right ahead,' he said, leaning on his stall, getting comfortable.

'Where were you Friday night?'

Timothy smiled widely.

'I went to see TrojKat at the GoTo with some of the Whitford Family. It was sick! Have you heard of her? I mean, I'm not into new music. I keep it 90s. But this was ace. Fresh!'

'Yes, I've heard of her,' said Norva through tight lips. 'I heard it was a great show.'

'It was. Memorable. I even went backstage for a bit.'

Norva looked disgusted.

'After that, I drove back to Brighton. I've just moved there. For the waves! Quick sleep, back to London early Saturday morning.'

'And back to Hugo,' Norva said. 'We think we know him pretty well – Nik especially – but you never know someone completely, do you?'

'Truth. That's deep.' Timothy nodded.

'Did he have any enemies? Was he arguing with anyone?' Norva continued.

He shook his head. 'Not that I know of. That man was well loved. Especially here. And he loved The Tri. Art Club was one of his favourite things.'

He patted me on the back. I appreciated it. I smiled up at him and looked over at Norva.

I raised my shoulders. She nodded her head in return.

'Well, thanks for your time, Timothy,' I said.

'Tim to you. If you're doing right by Hugo, you're good with me.' He high-fived us.

'See you next time,' said Norva.

We began to walk away.

Someone tripped over Ringo.

'Shorten that lead, please!' shouted a faceless person in the crowd.

'Oh, shut it!' Norva snapped, at nobody in particular.

'Oh wait!' Tim called to us. 'Time – that reminds me! Hugo tell you about the Clock?'

'Huh,' Norva said as we doubled back. 'What clock?'

'I dunno which clock it was, but he was totally hyped about it, man. When I saw him on Tuesday, he said he had a buyer. He was keen to sell it.'

'Can you tell us anything about it? Anything at all?' I asked.

'Nah, sorry, I just sell fabrics; I don't know anything about pieces of time. All I know is he said it was a 'seminal' and that it was going to change his fortune. He could pay back what he owed.'

'Pay back what he owed? To who? Was he in debt?' I said, interest piqued.

He shrugged. 'Maybe. He mentioned something about a charity woman with a Triangle.'

'The Tri-Angels?' we asked in unison to correct

him.

'Yeah, probably that.'

Jane. Noted.

Norva and I exchanged excited glances. The sandwiches might be expensive at Whitford Market, but the information was priceless.

We were done here. We thanked Timothy and rejoined the horde, squealing in excitement.

A lead!

'Wait, Norva, let me update our to-dos while they're fresh,' I shouted over to her.

She nodded and pointed to a doorway. Bright white pillars, a racing green front door. She slumped against it.

I tapped at my phone.

```
Motive: Money? Money for the clock?
To-do: Find out about the clock!
```

'What is this clock?' I said to Norva. 'There are so many clocks in the world – where do we even start?'

Norva shrugged. 'Dunno yet. But we need to, pretty quickly too. If it's worth anything – and it seems it is – that's our motive right there.' She danced on the spot. 'Motivations!' she sang, as she tapped her foot and shrugged her shoulders.

I nodded. 'I suppose so. Also, in other news: Hugo owed Jane money? For what? Why? That's a huge massive motive right there,' I shuddered. 'Jane. Creeping around our flat.'

'I know, right!' replied Norva, still dancing. 'I assumed Hugo was rolling in it; that's a shocker.'

'When you assume,' I said. 'You make an ass out of u and me. Hugo taught me that.'

~~To-do: Whitford Market~~

31

We decided to take flowers to Serena, but buying flowers from Whitford Market was clearly out of our budget. The World's Most Expensive Cheese Sandwich had made that crystal clear. Instead, Norva liberated some drooping carnations from a square adjacent to the market.

'They're on their way out – I'm doing a public service, my civic duty!' she protested.

I shielded her from the crowd while she pulled them from the ground. She tied the bunch together with her black hair tie and thrust them at me.

We walked to Serena's, at an undesirably slow pace. Norva dragged her feet across the pavement.

'That gardening job has tired me out. I'm almost too hungry for life.'

Ringo was hungry too. He attempted to eat the flowers. How could a dog be such a pig? I held the flowers high above my head.

'How long's Serena been on The Tri now?' asked Norva.

'Eighteen weeks. Why?'

'Ah, just considering her impact. She caught all the wasted fruit and unleashed the juice you're so hype about. She helped out with Hugo's art classes. The dog walking.'

'She also started that yoga class. And the Facebook group,' I added.

'Does she even have a job? Like a real one?'

'It doesn't seem so.'

'We should ask her about that. Where are the coins coming from, Serena?'

'Might be from her divorce?'

'Let's ask her.'

I nodded.

'Anyhow, yeah, she's done quite a bit around The Tri. She's alright that Serena,' Norva said, as if she just came to that decision. Perhaps she did.

'Yes, I do like her. She's quite impressive,' I said. 'I was hoping we would all be friends. Like what we had with Katie.'

Norva pursed her lips.

'I wouldn't go that far, to be honest,' she said, 'but she's alright.'

We knocked on Serena's door and waited.

Norva pressed her ear to it and shook her head.

'Don't think she's in.' As we began to walk away, the door opened behind us.

'Thank you, Serena, I'll send Officer Smyth up to see you shortly. We're all so sorry for your loss.'

A now-familiar voice.

DCI Sharp stood in the doorway.

She stared at us; we stared back.

'Hello, you two,' she said coldly. Thawing slightly, she added, 'I'd like to talk to you, and to thank you for being...somewhat sensible yesterday. This must be hard for you. I'm sorry for your loss.'

I shot a look at Norva.

'Yes it is, it's terrible,' said Norva. 'Terrible.'

DCI Sharp smiled, pursing her lips and walked away towards the lift.

'Hello, girls,' said Serena, leaning on her doorframe. Her green eyes were red-rimmed; her face was puffed and blotchy.

She'd been crying, and crying hard.

I didn't know what to say.

I held the flowers out to her. She took the bunch and sniffed them deeply.

'Thank you both, these are just darling.'

Serena inspected the black hairband holding them together.

'You know, I don't normally like flowers. It feels so wrong to cut something so beautiful and alive down in its prime. So sad.'

'I'm so sorry. Next time we'll bring you a plant,' I offered.

She laughed. 'Well, hopefully, there won't be another tragedy. She reached out her arms and we hugged.

'Come on in,' she said.

The flat smelled of a blend of fermenting fruit, fresh paint and dusty antiques. We passed an empty room, its door ajar. It was painted in the ever-present Tri yellow. Ringo pushed the door open with his nose. He strutted into the room and sat in the sun, making himself at home.

Serena laughed.

'Ringo is absolutely my favourite dog on The Tri. Bar none.'

'What's with the room? Ant infestation?' asked Norva.

'Yah!' said Serena, surprised. 'How did you know?'

'Ah, you know, all that fruit you're juicing, plus the sun, equals ants.'

'Yah, you're right, Norva.' She looked around the sparse room. 'Gosh, I miss my brother.'

Ringo yawned. Not appropriate. Norva apologetically tiptoed into the room to grab him. She shut the door behind her.

Serena led us to the living room.

Not that you could do much living in there.

It was crammed full of antiques, paintings, ornaments. Sympathy cards and flowers from residents lined all the available surfaces.

'Come sit,' Serena said.

'Where though?' asked Norva. 'I can barely breathe in here,' she whispered to me under her breath.

'Next to me on the chaise lounge, sillies.' Serena popped up behind a small sofa/bed hybrid and patted it.

Dust particles flew into the air. A heavy-looking trunk sat in front of it. Norva nudged it with her foot in an attempt to make space. It wouldn't budge.

'No, let me,' offered Serena. She pulled at the trunk with one arm. It slid across the floor with ease.

172

I perched on the trunk, between the 'sofa' and a tall stack of magazines. They had names like Antique Collecting and The Antiques Magazine. Clear descriptive names, I thought. You knew what you were getting.

'So how are you, and how's your father?' Serena asked. She smiled when she mentioned Pap.

I leaned forward to sneak a glance at Norva. She flicked her eyes toward me. Norva caught it too.

'I just want to be very clear with you,' Serena said sternly. 'Very clear. Your dad is a good man. He wouldn't do this.'

'Yeah, well, tell my sister that,' Norva said.

I spun my head round to look at her, exasperated.

Serena continued, 'Our neighbours are wrong. We have a security problem here. Who knows who comes and goes?'

I shook my head. 'That's not entirely true − there are cameras across The Tri. There might not be many, but they're strategically placed. Pap is definitely aware of most movements.'

'Yeah, we definitely know who comes and goes around here,' added Norva.

Serena looked at us quizzically. She sat back.

I changed the subject, quickly.

'Pap's OK, thanks for asking. He's upset about Hugo – obviously – and his leg is hurting a bit.'

'Oh, I noticed that on Saturday. I offered him a deep tissue massage, but he wanted to concentrate on work.'

'Oh, you did, did you?' said Norva, perking up, a hint of suspicion in her voice. 'When Saturday?'

'Saturday morning, bright and early! Eight AM.' Serena replied. 'He was here all day. Well, most of it.'

'Doing what?' I asked.

'Didn't he tell you? He and that lovely young chap he works with, Martin—'

'It's Mark,' Norva interjected tightly.

'Apologies, Mark, were working on Hugo's room on Saturday. Hugo arranged it aeons ago. They cleaned the room to—' She looked at Norva, nodding, '—get rid of the ants, and repainted it. I spent the day in the kitchen. The heat was ravishing my fruit – absolutely spoiling it – so I made a huge batch of juice. I handed it over to Sissy before it went to waste.'

I reached for my phone.

'So Pap was here all of Saturday. Painting with Mark, and he was limping?'

'Yah,' she replied. 'Such a good man. Working through the pain.'

32

'So, how well do you know Mark? I asked Serena.

Norva stared at her.

'Not very well at all…' she said. She looked down. 'I've seen him around, in the lifts, in the gardens. Sometimes walking around outside these three flats. And he's knocked here too, to buy Vitonica, direct from the source.' She smiled. 'But so many people do. I've had a very steady stream of visitors since I lost Hugo.' She gestured towards the cards. 'It's almost too difficult to keep faces and names straight.'

Serena looked out of the window.

'When did you see Hugo last, Serena? What happened after the meeting? Where did you go?' Norva asked.

I sat poised, phone in hand.

'I didn't really see him after the meeting. We came home, just after ten-thirty. The lifts were broken and after that climb, I was exhausted. I went to bed. I thought I heard something around one-fifteen, but I rolled back to sleep.'

'One-fifteen?' I asked. I stared at Norva.

Mrs K's friend left at that time.

Norva stared back.

Was the time of death window closing?

'Yah, around that time. I thought Hugo went to meet his girlfriend,' she said quietly.

'Girlfriend!?' Norva and I shouted in unison.

'Sorry, Serena.' Norva lowered her voice. 'Hugo's girlfriend? Who's that?'

'Well, I'm not certain they were seeing each other in that way, but I think it's the Chief Tri-Angel. Julie?' Serena replied.

'You mean Jane?' I asked.

'Yah, her.'

Hugo and Jane? Really?

'Are you sure?' asked Norva. 'They don't seem like, you know, they're a match. To me anyway.'

'You could never know with Hugo,' she said, waving her hand around the room.

'Could Hugo and Jane be talking about something else?' I offered. 'Antiques? Architecture?' I paused. 'Money?'

Serena turned sharply to me. 'Do you think so? Might it be about money?' She asked, eagerly. Norva looked at her, pursing her lips.

'I do hope not, because I don't have any money to give her!' She looked at her hands.

'Do you have a job?' I asked. 'Besides Vitonica, the dog walking and, you know, yoga?'

She shook her head. 'No, not really. I don't have a lot of money – not until my divorce is settled and the house in West London is sold. Hugo covered costs. Now he's gone, I'll have to go too, I'm sure.'

I reached for her hand. 'I hope not.'

Norva rolled her eyes.

'Me too.' Serena laughed bitterly.

I winced. It sounded like a cry.

'I'm having a rotten run of things,' she said. 'This year's been too hard, and now this place is full of bad energy. Bad vibes. I think my time – and work – here is done, girls. In trying to find myself, I lost my brother.'

Norva sat forward. 'Speaking of finding what you're looking for, Serena, have you heard about The Clock?'

Serena stood up. 'You know about The Clock?' she shouted. 'What do you know about it?

We sat back. Eyes wide.

'Wait there!' she said. 'Don't move!'

Serena tore out of the room.

'Oh my days,' Norva mouthed to me. 'What the hell is this now?'

'I don't know,' I whispered back. 'But I don't like it!'

Serena paced back into the room, knocking over the stack of magazines.

'Look!' She said, thrusting a crumpled piece of paper under our noses. 'Look!'

Norva reached for it.

'It was shoved under my door last night!'

A note. A4 white paper. Hand written, terribly. It read:

Tick! Tock! Tick! Tock!
Give Me The Flipping Clock
You're time runs out on Friday.

Serena was being threatened.

I gulped.

Norva's hands shook.

Motive: Money? Money for the clock? The Clock.

I took a photo.

'Did you show this to Sharp Shooter?' Norva asked.

'The Detective,' I clarified.

'Of course.'

'And she didn't take it from you? For evidence?' I asked.

'No, she looked at it and took a photo, like you.'

I looked back at the note. One thing bothered me. Irrationally.

'You're?'

'I know,' said Serena.

To-do: Find out who wrote Serena's note

'Hugo has so many things,' Serena said, sitting down. 'A myriad of clocks and other timepieces. Do you know which one they could be talking about? Where do I start?'

We shook our heads.

I shrugged.

'I'm not sure. We just have a feeling that this one was special to him, and important. Valuable,' I said.

'Clearly,' she replied. 'Take a look around – see if anything jumps out at you. Let's also swap numbers, so you can let me know immediately if you find out more.'

Serena tapped our numbers into her phone.

'Have you looked in his van, since, since…?' I asked, my question trailing away.

She shook her head. 'No. I don't have the keys. I have no idea where they'd be.' Her eyes filled with tears. 'I hope I find this clock. For my own safety, obviously, but I'd like to give it to our father. If it was so special to him, it would be priceless for Daddy…' She coughed back a cry.

I touched her shoulder. 'That's a lovely thought, Serena. We're on the case.'

She held my hand.

'Thank you, girls. You are just darling.'

33

We sat in silence.

'Ohh!' Serena said. 'I need to pop to the loo,' she said and dabbed at her eyes.

As she ducked into to her bathroom, I shouted after her: 'Can I have a juice, please?'

'Afraid not, I don't have any at the moment. No time – or desire – to make them,' Serena called back.

Understandably.

We stood up, looked around the living room, being careful not to break anything.

We stepped into the kitchen.

'Hugo and *Jane*?' Norva whispered. 'Crazy if correct, but no chance! Hugo's gay. She's his sister, she should know that!'

'Yep. She should,' I replied. 'Also – Pap's limp.'

Norva slumped against the fridge. 'What about it? He got it between Friday night and Saturday morning.'

'I know. I figured that out too. I hope he didn't get it at one-fifteen, when someone, possibly Kowalski's 'friend', was moving around.'

Norva stared at me.

'And speaking of moving around, why is Mark everywhere? He has no reason to be walking around outside Serena's flat – he's not friends with George and Nina, or Jane is he?'

Norva shrugged. 'Doubt it.'

'I don't think he knew Hugo well either.'

I moved Norva out of the way of the fridge and pulled open the door. 'Norva – there's loads of juice in here, but it looks off. That must be what she meant about not having any.'

I took a photo and shut the door, looking around the rest of the kitchen:

     • One juicer

     • Three large piles of cherries, apples and bananas

     • A tub of sealed Tupperware with fruit pulp, cherry seeds, peach pits, almonds and other unconfirmed nuts

'Sealed to keep it from the ants?' I asked Norva. She shrugged. 'Possibly. Take a photo.'

I didn't need to be told.

Over at the bin, under the sink, was a crumpled bag of fast food.

'Dirty food for such a seemingly clean person,' Norva laughed.

I moved back to the worktop next to the fridge. Attached to its side was a pin board, and attached to the board were various notes and a calendar.

I peered at it closely. This Friday's date was circled in thick red pen. Next to the number was a crude symbol. A clock icon.

'Norva,' I called. She peered at it. 'Looks like a pie to me. Friday Pieday. God, I'm so hungry.'

'That's not a pie, come on! That's the international symbol for a clock!'

I took a photo and searched the pin board.

- Dry cleaning tickets
- Shopping lists
- Hugo's passport photo

'They should have used that one at the market,' Norva said. 'It's way more flattering.'

• A rectangle of paper with names and a sum of money written on it.

I nudged Norva and took a photo.

'That's a cheque, Nik,' she said. 'PayPal for olds.'

This cheque was addressed to 'Tri-Angels Ltd'. £250 cheque from Hugo C Knightley-Webb. The line that had the word 'signature' next to it was blank.

'Hugo *did* owe Jane money?' I said.

'And so much! Why isn't it signed? Why doesn't Jane have it?' said Norva. 'Are you telling me Serena hasn't seen this cheque before?'

I shrugged. 'Seems unlikely.'

'What's her deal?' she whispered.

'Whose deal?' said Serena, appearing suddenly behind us.

We jumped.

'Oh...' I said, stumped for something to say. I looked at the juicer. 'How you could supply all that Vitonica with just one juicer?'

Norva jumped in brightly. 'Yeah, what's the deal with that?' she laughed, raising her hands.

'Ah, you know. I just work hard,' Serena said with a smile.

34

We let ourselves into our flat. Ringo ran ahead. He lapped loudly at the water in his bowl.

Pap was home early. His dirty, large boots were by the door. I picked up a shoe and turned it over to examine it.

It was flecked in dried yellow paint. Tri-Yellow.

I set the boot back gently on the floor, sole up, reached for my phone and took a picture. The flash lit up the hall. Norva shook her head.

'Are you going to shake your head at me every time I do something? I'm getting tired of it. I'm being thorough,' I hissed.

'I'll shake my head at who and what I like,' she replied.

We walked through the lounge into the kitchen. Pap was at the sink, his back to us. I sat at the table.

Norva headed straight for the fridge. She threw a Vitonica at me, which I caught like a cricketer. She tore into a pack of smoked ham, which she ate in fistfuls.

'Alright, Pap?' Norva asked him between mouthfuls. 'Why you home so early?'

No reply.

'Pap?' I asked.

'I was sent home from first aid training,' he said with a sigh. 'They'd heard the news, and watched the Cloud News report. They said I was a distraction.'

I looked at Norva. Ham hung from her mouth.

'Where have you been all morning?' he asked us in a low voice.

The lie jumped out.

'Ah, we've been with George. Out and about.'

He turned around. His face was soft. 'Yeah? Good. Hope you had a fun one. Potato salad and cold cuts for lunch, alright?'

We nodded.

'If there's any left, that is.' Pap glanced at Norva, winced and limped over to the fridge.

It was time to know.

'Pap,' I started gently. 'What happened to your leg?'

'Ah, I pulled it on Friday night.'

I sipped on my juice nervously. Norva stopped chewing.

'After the meeting?' I tried to sound natural and light. Nonchalant.

He looked at us.

'Yes. I was getting rid of some rubbish. On the way back, I wasn't watching where I was going and hit my leg hard on an open door.'

I felt cold in the heat. I left the table to join Pap at the sink. He was distracted and fidgety, vigorously washing yellow from his hands. I looked up at him.

'I can't get this paint off my hands!' He rubbed his hands under the water.

'You'll catch fire if you don't dial back that friction, Pap,' Norva said.

He smiled and turned off the tap.

'Is that the Tri paint?' I asked.

Norva mouthed, 'Stop it!'

'The one and only,' he replied.

'Who's getting work done at the moment, Pap? In Corner One? I know George's mum wanted to refresh her kitchen.'

The lie flowed out.

'Hugo and Serena were done this weekend,' he said. 'Me and Mark took care of that. That Mark is struggling. Very broke, poor kid. Literally. Mrs Kowalski,' he looked down, 'was finished around the same time.'

'When exactly?' I asked.

'Ah, over the weekend,' he said, with a dismissive wave of his hand.

So that's where Norva gets it from.

'Where were you painting today, then?'

'When I got back I did some little touch ups. Had another go at the burn in The Hub. It just won't go.' He shook his head.

'So what about Nina?' I asked. 'Maybe Norva and I could have some paint and work on her kitchen?'

'No chance,' muttered Norva.

'No. Sorry,' said Pap. 'That paint is managed by me and me only. Nina will have to join the back of the queue. I can't just push everyone up the list. There is a system. There are rules.'

So that's where I get it from.

Pap sighed. 'I'll get into more trouble if I don't follow it.'

'What trouble? What's going on, Pap?' I said gently, my arms around his waist. Norva started making lunch by putting food onto plates and not directly into her mouth.

'Everyone – and I mean everyone – is talking about me and Hugo.' He sighed. 'I'll be honest, he could be a right fool. And I know he owes Jane some money, but he didn't deserve this. No one does. Ever. It got hot at the meeting, sure, but we made up. It was all cool. Or so I thought.'

'You made up with Hugo?' Norva asked.

'Yeah, I dropped him a note and apologised. He replied and accepted it.'

'What note?' I added.

'I emailed him. Said sorry. I was rude. I can't excuse that behaviour.'

I reached for my phone.

Pap apologized to Hugo via email.

'Do you remember the time?' I asked.

'Probably Eleven-thirty ish?'

I updated the file. His anger with Hugo had faded, but that didn't mean he was in the clear.

'Where did Hugo go on Friday after the meeting? Did you see him?' Norva asked as she set the table.

'Nah. I'd normally run into him on a Sunday on Third Avenue, coming back from Bermuda's. I didn't see him this Sunday, for reasons now obvious.'

'We saw Serena today,' I said. 'She told us Hugo had a girlfriend.'

Pap roared with laughter. 'Hahaha! Nope. No.'
He laughed again. 'Serena said that? Hugo? A girlfriend?'

'That's what we thought. We thought he was gay.'

Pap nodded.

'But Serena thought he was seeing Jane.'

Pap stopped laughing. 'Jane? Really? Hugo and
Jane were definitely not together. At least as far as I
know. I'm pretty certain about that.'

'How can you be so sure?' I asked.

Pap looked down at the table. 'I just know about
these things,' he said.

I glanced at Norva. A disgusted look slowly crept
over her face. She was reaching the same conclusion as
me.

The arm touching.

The sandwiches.

Recognising her in the dark.

Pap and Jane.

What! He's had girlfriends after mum, sure.

But her? Jane?

I looked back at Norva. She was touching her
neck and gagging. I swallowed hard, and changed the
subject, somewhat.

'How did you know that Hugo owed her
money?' I said.

'Ah, I talk to Jane about a lot of things.' Norva retched. Pap saw. 'Tri-Angel stuff. I put their plans into action for them,' he said, quickly.

'Oh,' I said. 'So was that who you were talking to on the phone? Yesterday, when we told you about Hugo?'

'Tri-Angel stuff?' said Norva.

'Yeah, something like that,' he said, avoiding the topic. 'Let's eat, OK?'

```
To-do: Ask Pap about his conversation and
limp
```

We sat down.

'So did you get a massage from Serena then?' Norva asked.

'Excuse me?' shouted a shocked Pap. He put down his fork.

Norva smiled. 'Your limp? She said she could have sorted your leg out?'

'Oh, oh right. Yes. No, I was too busy for that,' he said. 'Me and Mark were there all day. Serena was mostly on the phone. Talking a whole lot.'

'Did you sort out the ants?'

'Nope – that job's out of my remit. I gave pest

control a ring, and sorted out an appointment for her. We were just refreshing Hugo's bedroom. *That* job's been on the list for ages. He booked it months ago.'

'Did you see his clock?' Norva asked.

'His what?' said Pap.

'The clock,' I said. 'It was one of Hugo's favourite things,' I said.

Pap shrugged. 'Have you seen the state of their place? I wouldn't know what I was looking at.'

I looked through the files on my phone.

'Pap. Mrs Kowalski said a friend was helping her out on Friday night. Did you see anyone when you were…getting rid of rubbish?'

'Kowalski said that?' he asked.

I nodded.

'So, did you do it together?' I asked.

Pap slammed his fist on the table. We jumped. My juice went flying, splashing onto the plate of meat. Ringo yelped. He ran straight out of the kitchen and probably into my bed.

'Do it together?' he shouted. 'Did we kill Hugo? Is that what you mean?'

'No, no! Pap, that's not what I meant. Not at all! I was wondering if you were helping her. That's all! I'm sorry!'

Pap put his head in his hands and rubbed his face.

'I'm sorry for shouting, Nik, I'm so sorry.' He extended a hand to me, and I took it.

He gazed out of the window.

'I'm just so tense. Everyone's talking about me. Everyone. They're whispering about me all over The Tri. I can feel the eyes all over me – everywhere I go. I saw The Cloud News report. And just last night, when you were asleep, Katie's boss was here. Her team are crawling all over my office. I got sent home from work. It's too much.'

He turned to look at us.

'And now it seems you're getting caught up in an investigation of your own? Please don't. Stop. I need you to be safe!'

He picked at the ham on his plate and chewed it slowly.

We ate the rest of our lunch in silence. I choked back potato salad. I couldn't look at Pap. Or Norva.

I knew she'd have choice words for me shortly.

35

'That was well tense!' I said, faking a light laugh. I didn't know what else to say.

I shut our bedroom door.

Norva turned to me with furious eyes.

'What are you doing?' she said, her mouth tense.

'Trying to solve the case?' I said. My heart pounded. 'Facts, evidence, deduction.'

'I know of someone who needs deducting from this family. And it ain't Pap,' Norva said through gritted teeth.

Her words stung. My chest ached. My eyes filled with tears.

'Norva, I was actually trying to help, I think…'

'You know what I think?' Norva cut in. 'I think you're pinning this on Pap. You. Just. Won't. Stop. What will it take for you to quit it? It's beyond a bad look at this point. It's disgusting. You're disgusting right now.'

'Norva, I'm really not framing Pap. I don't want him to go to prison, do I!?'

I started to cry.

'Doesn't seem like it to me,' Norva said with a sneer.

'I'm trying to rule him out! What if he was with Kowalski on Friday, doing their project, whatever that was? He'd be out of the picture! I'm trying to help!'

I lay on my bed and sobbed into my pillow.

'I'm just being methodological. Procedural. Like the detectives you love on TV,' I said, mainly to the pillow.

Norva sat on my bed. I felt a hand on my back.

'I'm sorry, Nik,' she said. 'I know. But it isn't TV, is it? It's real life. The literal definition of 'close to home'. Dictionary.com would have our faces next to that entry, girl.'

I laughed and wiped my eyes.

Norva stood up and looked out of the window. She stared across The Tri.

'I get what you're doing,' she said, her back to me. 'And I know it seems like I'm trying to stop you. I am, basically. I. Am. Freaking. Out. I'm screaming internally. Have been since we found Hugo. Don't think I'm not.'

'That's why we need to look at what we have so far,' I said. 'We have to stay in control. And keep going.'

Norva nodded.

I wiped my eyes and reached for my phone. Hugo's lid was also in my pocket. I forgot about that. My thumb stroked it as I went through the notes.

'Pap said he's apologised to Hugo and Hugo replied. We need to find that email, somehow.' Norva nodded.

'You're right. I'll try and snatch Pap's phone later. The timings on those emails will be mad important.'

'We can also see what websites he may have been on, check his location, see who he's been texting.'

To-do: Get Pap's phone

'I think we know who he's been texting,' said Norva.

'Jane,' I replied. 'It makes sense.' I flicked through my photos. 'Look at the way she's touching him on Monday.' I showed her the photo of them outside the bins. She shuddered.

'Also — it explains how she was able to get into our flat when the door was locked.'

'Eurgh, she has a key to ours?'

I nodded. 'Seems so.'

'How long has this been going on?' she wailed. 'Ick, nasty, I hate it.'

'Can't say I'm a fan either. But now we know why he was so certain Hugo wasn't seeing her. Because he was.'

'Yuck, yuck, yuck,' spat Norva. 'Disa-flipping-prove!'

'Now you know how I feel about you and Mark,' I said, with a smile.

'Not the same. Not at all. Mark's moody, cool and strong.'

'How strong? Strong enough to move a body?'

Norva was silent. She shrugged. 'Maybe so. Let's go back out.'

I agreed. I reached for my trainers. 'I'm sorry to say this, but Mark has a motive – he thinks Hugo has money, Serena's seen him around the flats and…'

'Hold up!' Norva said suddenly, cutting me off and leaning down to look in the telescope.

'What? Who can you see?'

She was silent.

'Norva!' I demanded.

'What are they doing together?' she hissed.

'Norva – who are you talking about?' I ran to

the window and pushed her away from the telescope. I refocused the lens. Below, Mark and Serena were walking across The Tri.

Mark was sipping a Vitonica. Lucky. Serena was talking, walking quickly to match his pace. She smiled up at him.

I watched them disappear into the lobby of Corner One.

'What's that about?'

'I don't know, but I don't like it. At all,' Norva said, crossing her arms.

36

'I'm over Mark, you know. He's well distracting and I gotta focus. I'm done.'

'Hope so,' I replied, knowing that she'd be 'done' for about four hours. Maximum.

'That's for the best. We're too young for 'love' anyway. Now our priorities are in the correct order.'

We put Ringo on his lead.

'Bye Pap!' I shouted down the hall. 'Just walking Ringo, OK?'

Pap looked back at us. 'Absolutely – as long as you promise to keep yourselves to yourselves?'

I didn't dare look at Norva. I simply nodded.

'Sure Pap' said Norva. 'Of course.'

And we were gone.

'When Mark gets out of this lift, I'll do the talking,' said Norva. 'I'm ready to ask questions, dig deep.'

'I'm sure you are,' I replied.

The lift arrived. It was empty.

'Hmm,' said Norva. 'Maybe he's at Serena's then?'

We got in.

The three flats on Third Avenue had identical red doors. I knocked on Serena's. No answer.

'Where did they go then?' I asked Norva. She narrowed her eyes. 'Not here, evidently. Maybe The Hub?'

I leant over the Avenue and looked across The Tri. A quiet afternoon. Hot, again. Thirty-two degrees.

'Where is everyone?' I said.

Norva shrugged. 'Calm before the storm, probably.'

I looked at her quizzically. 'What do you mean?'

'I don't know. Something stirring in my waters. Also, I just like saying it. Ignore me.'

Good advice. I took it.

I turned to look back at the flats, the three red doors and their doormats. I rolled my eyes at George's.

'Welcome Bach,' I scoffed.

'Don't hate, it's on-brand at least,' said Norva.

I looked closer at the walkway around the mats. Yellow boot-prints.

'Norva look,' I pointed. I crouched to take a closer look. 'I didn't notice these earlier.'

The footprints were large. Much bigger than our feet, at least. The prints looked fresh. Mostly. I touched one and a small amount of paint stuck to my fingertip.

'Mildly tacky,' I whispered.

'Yeah, like you,' laughed Norva.

'Funny.' I looked up at her. 'These prints look familiar, Norva.'

'I bet,' she said wearily.

I reached for my phone. I took a photo. I flicked back between the new photo and the photo of Pap's boots.

A match. Of course.

I pushed my phone in Norva's face and switched between the photographs. She dismissed me.

'Sure, they're Pap's. But so what? He was here Saturday. Painting. We been knew. Old intel.'

'But these are fresh, Norva.' I said.

'He was painting today, though,' she replied.

'Yeah, but at The Hub, not up here.'

I was silent.

'Alright, I hear you,' she said. 'Even if he was lying, which he wasn't, what do fresh prints prove? At this point?'

'I don't know Norva,' I said, desperately. 'But the police might probably match these to Pap's and draw incorrect conclusions.'

Norva nodded. 'Maybe.'

'What if someone's trying to frame him?' I added. 'This could be a good way to do it.'

'Maybe. Let's see where they lead.'

```
To-do: Find out why Pap's bootprints were on
Third Avenue
```

We walked between the flats and the chute. Back and forth. The prints were everywhere.

We followed them from George's flat to the chute. From Serena's to the chute. From Jane's flat to the chute.

'What the hell is this?' said Norva. 'This is wack! Didn't realise Pap was so freaking messy. He's out here like a pre-schooler with a potato stamp!'

'He's not messy,' I said. 'This can't be him. He was at the first aid course this morning. What is this?'

We walked back to the chute. It was out-of-order, of course. Cordoned off, covered in blue and white police tape. Katie's work, probably.

'Still hums bad, even with, you know, Hugo

gone,' Norva said. 'And now it's part of the crime scene, it won't be cleared for at least a week, I'm guessing.'

'Or until they've made an arrest,' I replied.

Norva nodded. 'This is the only time I've been glad we don't have the chute on 22,' she said. 'This stench would end me.'

It was foul.

'The tenants deserve a discount,' I said.

Norva laughed. 'No chance.'

There was a camera hanging above the Avenue, pointed at the chute.

Norva peered at it. 'What's the time Mr Wolf?' she asked, staring into it.

'14:37. Why?'

No answer. She took down her braids, flicked them side to side and gave the camera a peace sign. She made an idiotic kissing face.

'Really, Norva?'

'Alright, alright. I'm done, I'm done,' she said, holding her hands up. 'Timeline marked.'

She ducked under the Police tape and opened the chute. As it creaked open, a strong cloud of stench wafted up.

'Hello!' Norva shouted into the void. She breathed in the fug, and immediately gasped.

'Regrets,' she said, between coughs.

We looked into the chute and down into the refuse area.

'Oi!' Officer Burnett shouted up at us. 'You're officially trespassing. This is a murder scene, and you know it.'

'So sorry, officer!' Norva shouted. 'Our mistake!'

Ringo barked, backing up Norva.

Officer Burnett's radio buzzed nosily, and he reached for it.

The voice at the other end was garbled to us, but the message was very clear to him.

'Copy that. Over,' he said, walking briskly away. We ran to the lift.

37

Pap was deep in conversation with Jane outside The Hub.

'Eurgh,' said Norva. 'Let's break this cozy couple up. I'm gonna ask him about those prints.'

We skipped over.

'...you need to tell them, Jane, what if they...'

Their conversation ended abruptly.

'Ayy, Pap,' Norva addressed him with a smile. 'Jane,' she said coldly, looking her up and down, pursing her lips. 'Alexanders Assemble, Pap? We gotta chat. Real talk time.'

'Alright,' he said. He looked to Jane. 'We'll continue this conversation later, OK?'

Jane nodded, seemingly exasperated.

She walked away.

'That's right, off you pop,' said Norva under her breath.

Pap turned to us. 'Good timing, actually,' he said. 'I need to come clean about Frid…' he started.

He didn't finish.

A deafening siren wailed and screamed at us. Lights blinked brightly in the afternoon sun. The police had returned to The Tri, and oh, what an entrance.

A car screeched to a jerking halt in front of us, three rabbits in the blue lights.

The car door opened and Katie stepped out. She put her hat on and smoothed her uniform. She walked over to us, her fists clenched. She bit into her lip. Her eyes were red.

My heart fell through my chest and settled in my stomach.

'Katie,' Norva whispered quietly. 'No. Don't. Please.'

'Joseph Alexander?'

'Erm, Yes?' Pap replied. Confused. Slightly laughing, 'You know who I am, Katie.'

Katie closed her eyes. A tear rolled down her face. She took a deep breath. Her eyes opened. She focused.

'Joseph Alexander. You are being arrested on suspicion of the murder of Hugo Knightley-Webb. You have the right to remain silent, anything you say can be...'

Pap's face fell.

Katie's voice faded away, and my ears rang.

My stomach rose into my chest, through my throat and into my mouth.

Norva dropped to her knees. Her eyes were wild, wide open. Shock and terror.

The scene unfolded around us in slow motion. People leaned out of their windows. People rushed out of Bermuda's and Better Buy. People surrounded us. They held their phones high in the air, capturing every single moment.

I grabbed Norva's hand and she gripped mine in return.

The shouting began.

'Joe – wha ya do?'

'He merked Hugo for real?'

'Nah, I'm not having this! Joe would never!'

From the left: *'Stay schtum Joe. Not a word. We got you!'*

The right: *'Knew it –Sasha you owe me a score.'*

Another: *'Sissy called it!'*

Officer Burnett, who was standing next to Katie, stepped forward. He unclipped a pair of handcuffs and slipped them on Pap's waiting wrists.

Pap was silent, shocked and stern.

Officer Burnett walked Pap to the car. He pushed his head down. He pushed him into the back seat.

'I'm innocent!' Pap screamed. 'I'm innocent!' He shouted from the back of the car.

He kicked the seat in front of him.

'Joe say nothing, calm down!' shouted a voice behind us. 'Don't upset the feds!'

Pap stopped struggling immediately.

'Jane?' His eyes scanned the crowd.

'Jane!' He found her. 'Get the girls!'

I turned to see Jane nodding frantically behind me. She blinked in shock and terror.

'Girls – my place. Now.' She pushed her way through the crowd.

Officer Burnett slammed the passenger door and sat in the driver's seat. Ringo jumped at the window. His frantic paws clawed and scratched at the paintwork.

Pap looked at us, and down into his lap. The car screeched away.

Norva remained on the ground. Her left knee bled slightly. She held a weak grip on Ringo's lead as he licked at her face, concerned. She looked up at me.

'I should have taken you more seriously,' she said.

38

All of the eyes on The Tri focused on Norva and me. I pulled her to her feet.

'We need to go. Now.'

Tears fell down her face as Norva stood up. She brushed her dress off, wiped her eyes and threw her head back.

'You're right. They can't see me like this.' She held her nose in the air. Back straight. The crowd parted, silently. I turned to look at them. They stared at us. Phones aloft.

May Burton from Cloud News appeared with her camera crew.

'No comment!' Norva screamed at her.

Not now. Not ever.

I pushed Norva and Ringo into the lobby of Corner One. My heart pounded. I burst into tears.

'You were right, Nik!' Norva said.

I wiped my eyes.

'About Pap being the 'obvious' suspect? Considering the evidence, that was clear. We both knew this. I just accepted it, I suppose.'

'I need to ask you – be straight with me. Do you think he did this?' She stared in my eyes.

'Norva, I 100% don't,' I said, holding her gaze. 'Pap wouldn't do this. We know this. But we need to prove it. Belief is not enough.'

'So now, not only do we have to find Hugo's murderer, we also have to save our Dad?' she said.

I nodded. 'Yes.'

'Why did I wish for drama? Why?' She slapped her forehead. 'I'm such an idiot. I miss "The Missing Hat days".'

'Those are long gone, I'm afraid.'

'Innit though.'

I pointed up, towards our flat. She nodded. We moved toward the lift.

'Yes, Officer Symth, I know.' A familiar wintry voice murmured from Pap's office.

I pointed left, towards the Investigation Room. Norva nodded. We moved to the office door.

It was ajar again.

DCI Sharp had her back to us.

Katie was in profile, sitting at Pap's desk.

We listened in.

'Kathyrn – if I may. You are an...adequate officer. Your work here has been average to good. But you are trying your best. I can see that.'

'Thank you,' Katie replied, quietly.

Norva and I exchanged looks. That was barely a compliment.

'We're so up against it here – you know this – you've barely slept. Most of the Officers are still deployed North. There are three of us on this investigation. Three! That's unheard of. It's criminal.'

Katie sniffed. 'I know.'

'I understand you know and like *these people*...'

Norva raised her eyebrows. Her lips tightened.

'...and I needed you to experience an arrest, but nothing changes unless we get crystal clear evidence of his innocence by this time tomorrow. Otherwise, Mr Alexander will be charged with murder...'

Norva squealed. Her hands flew to her mouth to contain it.

Too late.

'...you know very well we can only hold a suspect for twenty-four hours. We need to wrap this up.'

Katie sobbed.

My eyes filled with tears.

'He threatened the victim's life – in front of multiple witnesses. We have it on video. He has a motive – the repairs over the statue. His key witness – when he finally admitted his whereabouts on Friday – won't corroborate. Add this to the paint can, the CCTV, those boot prints… He needs an alibi, Officer Smyth, and a strong one.'

Katie spoke up. 'It just doesn't make sense. He wouldn't. Joseph just wouldn't do this,' she protested. 'He just wouldn't.'

I'd heard enough. I stepped back and called the lift. It opened immediately.

Norva stuck her tongue out for the camera above and twisted her braids.

'This again? Now?' I whispered. 'Right now?'

'No, this is important,' she said.

We stepped in and Norva pushed the button marked 21. The lift was hot and slow.

I reached into my pockets. My fingers brushed against Hugo's lid.

I cried. Loud, deep sobs. Norva hugged me.

'We're officially pre-orphans,' she said, bursting into tears.

39

Jane's door was open. 'Jane?' Norva asked into the hall.

'Come on in, girls,' Jane shouted breathlessly from inside her home. She shuffled into view. 'Are you OK? Where are you staying tonight? Here?'

No chance. I didn't want to stay with Jane. She threw her arms around us, attempting a hug.

We recoiled and she stepped back, disappointed.

'No, Serena's staying with us,' Norva said.

I shot Norva a quizzical look. She nudged me in the ribs in return.

Jane ushered us into her hall. A neat line of shoes faced the wall.

She coughed and gently pointed to them. In response, I took my trainers off and placed them next to her shoes. Norva kicked off her sandals and left them where they lay, disrupting the row.

Jane's living room was pleasant. Just like her. Like a grandma's house is pleasant. Neat. Lace. Tablecloths. Painted yellow, obviously. Lavender scented. Pleasant.

Around her room:

• Twelve certificates, framed, on her walls, celebrating her fundraising efforts
• Fifteen photographs, framed, of Jane with vaguely recognisable people holding large cheques
• A slightly glamorous and misty portrait of Jane in her younger years, circa 1987

Jane's face beamed down at us, from every direction. Norva pointed to her portrait and stifled a laugh.

'Some water, girls?' Jane offered. She looked at me. 'I don't have any juice. Sorry. I find it too sickly sweet – a bit like its maker.'

Norva glanced at me.

'Yes, please,' I replied. 'Water would be great, thank you.'

We followed her through her lounge and into the kitchen.

'It's terrible about Joe – your Dad – I mean, sorry. While I was waiting for you, I put a plan together.' She motioned to a notepad on the table.

'Right – listen to this. I'll divert the funds The Tri-Angels raised for Mother's on The Moon. That gives us money to start building a legal defence. It's not a lot, but it's a start. That, plus savings, I reckon we can get us a decent lawyer. Not the best, but we can try. I've started looking on the internet and I...'

I kept my ears on the conversation, but used my eyes to look around her kitchen. It smelt of paint. Same layout as ours – just neater, brighter and fresher. Jane had clean, folded tea-towels on a shelf. What a thing.

Underneath her sink, I saw a boot. And then another. A pair of work boots. Large. Possibly Pap's? They were covered in yellow paint. Definitely Pap's.

I nudged Norva. Her eyes narrowed. How could they be here, when they were just at home?

I reached for my phone and looked through my photos. The shoes matched. I was sure of it. Were there two pairs of boots? Or more?

I attempted a stealthy photo but my subtle phone made an obvious sound. An old-school camera-flashing noise.

'What was that?' said Jane alarmed. 'Are you taking photos in here? Why? What are you taking photos of?' She said, walking towards us. We stepped backwards.

'No, no,' I stuttered.

'That's just her wack text tone,' Norva jumped in. 'Told you it was basic, yet confusing, didn't I?'

I nodded.

Jane laughed and raised her hands, in faked confusion.

'Young girls and your tech, can't keep up!' Her face softened. 'So, like I said, once the wire transfer comes through from the Embassy, we should be able to post bail − if it comes to that. Hopefully it doesn't. Obviously.'

'That's very kind of you, Jane,' Norva said. 'And maybe not entirely legal, but whatever… you're so generous with your money.'

Jane smiled. 'Well, it's not *my* money − it's Tri money, and this is a Tri-mergency.'

I groaned.

'I'm sorry, I can't help it,' she said.

'Do the Tri-Angels often lend money to people in need?' I asked.

'Sometimes – depending on the situation.'

'And does anyone owe The Tri-Angels any money?'

She looked down. 'No one 'owes' us money. But we we're waiting on a significant pledge. £250. But that's not going to come now.'

'Why not?' I asked.

'It's just no longer available,' she said with a sigh.

'That's such a sad coincidence,' Norva said.

'What is?' said Jane, looking up.

'We saw a cheque addressed to The Tri-Angels yesterday. For that exact amount. It wasn't signed though.'

'You did?' she said surprised and confused. Her voice was high.

We nodded. Then, she understood.

'Oh!' she whispered. 'He actually wrote the cheque?' She spoke softly. 'Wow, Hugo, you were serious?' She wept. 'You kept your word.'

'What word?' I asked her.

Jane sighed. 'Hugo kindly offered The Tri-Angels £250. Not for any statue, in particular. He said he was going to come into some real money soon – a life-changing amount. He wanted to make a promise to the community.'

Her eyes welled with tears.

'So very generous.' She looked me in the eye. 'But it's not worth any life. Not Hugo's life, my life. Or Joe's.'

'Did you trust Hugo?' I asked.

'Yes, I did,' she said, dabbing at her eyes. 'He was a bit artsy for me, always critiquing my Tri-Angels posters.' She laughed. 'But he was great. I loved him.'

'Like 'love' loved him?' asked Norva.

Jane laughed. 'No.'

'Oh, we must have got it wrong, sorry!' Norva replied.

Jane stopped laughing. 'What do you mean, "got it wrong"?'

'Oh, we just heard that you and Hugo were close. Real close,' Norva said, winking at me.

Jane was serious. 'Who's been telling fibs?'

'Are they 'fibs'?' asked Norva.

'Yes. Yes they are. I'm...' she looked down. 'In love with someone else.'

Norva shuddered, recoiled and stuck out her tongue.

'Now who told you this?' Jane demanded. 'Tell me!'

'Serena,' I said. 'It was Serena.'

Jane's face tightened. 'Figures.'

'Figures how?' I asked.

'I get the feeling Serena doesn't like me – or The Tri-Angels – very much. She thinks we're all a bit unsophisticated. Common.'

'So, on Friday night, after the meeting, you weren't with Hugo?' I asked for confirmation.

Tears sprung from Jane's eyes. 'I was not with Hugo! I was not. I was like this! Crying. Crying on my own.' She threw her hands in the air. 'This is such a mess.

She looked at us. 'Look, I know what you're trying to do. It wasn't me.'

'Why were you crying on Friday night?' I asked.

'I was waiting for a visitor. He never came.'

40

We told Jane we were staying at Serena's, but we crept home. We didn't want to be alone this evening, really, but we had no choice. There was no one we could fully trust – excluding each other.

'Potential murderers out here. Everywhere. Safest place is home,' said Norva. She put her key into the door.

Ding! Ding!

A text from Serena.

Girls! I heard about your Dad. Who is looking after you tonight? Come and stay with me!

Norva replied.

We turned on every light in the flat, and drew the curtains, even though the sun had only just begun to go down. We climbed into Pap's bed. Ringo lay between us.

'Pap would hate this. We're breaking all his rules,' I said.

'Rules, pffft,' Norva snorted. 'Rules are dead. The Tri is Anarchy HQ.'

'Sure is,' I replied. 'So much has happened today. Too much. And we've only got around 23 hours before it's too late.' I shuddered.

'Innit, I'll start in reverse order,' Norva said. I nodded, my phone in hand.

'Jane and Hugo are obviously not an item.'

'Obviously.'

'That means Serena's instincts are super messed up.'

I nodded. 'Understandably. She's been through a lot.'

'Jane's in love with Pap,' Norva said, shuddering. 'And knowing what we now know, he was supposed to be with her on Friday night.'

'Yep.'

'Do you think she's gonna try to be our step mum? Norva asked. 'Especially now?'

'I really hope not,' I said. 'But he didn't go – she was crying about it. So where was he? You heard DCI Sharp say the Friday Night Witness refuses to corroborate. Why?'

Norva shrugged. 'That's the key to this whole mess. Pap is clearly Mrs Kowalski 'friend'.'

'Almost certainly.'

'So why not just say that? What's the big deal?'

'I guess that depends on what the project was…' My voiced trailed off.

Norva stared at me. 'We need to get that intel out of her as a priority.'

I nodded. 'Pap's boots at Jane's,' I said, changing the subject. 'How many pairs *are* there?'

'Right? She must be the person making the prints. If so, why? What's the point?'

'To be determined. Mark and Serena,' I said. 'What were they doing walking across The Tri, and where did they go?'

Norva shut her eyes. 'Mark,' she sighed. 'What are you doing, my love?'

'My love? I thought you were 'done with him?''

I looked at my phone. Three hours and thirty minutes. Standard Norva.

'We need to talk to him. He's the only person we haven't spoken to in detail.'

'I don't know if I can take it,' Norva said.

'You need to take it and get on board quickly. Now Pap's absent and we know he didn't do it, we have to hone in on Mark.'

Norva gulped. 'You're right, you're right,' she said quietly. 'What else do we have to do?'

I searched back through our file. 'Other things to find out: Serena's note.'

'And The Clock,' said Norva. 'The motive.'

'The motive,' I repeated.

We looked up at the ceiling. Ringo yawned.

'Maybe we need to start some new documents.' I said, rolling over to face her. 'We could do with new checklists. To help us get through this. To be additionally thorough.'

'OK, how's this?' Norva sat up. 'Title. "Help! Your Dad's Been About To Be Charged With Murder".'

'Point one. Freak out. Check.

'Point two. Trust no one. Check.

'Point three. Figure it out. In progress.

'Point four. Set Dad free. Possibly.

'Point five. Live great lives. Uncertain.'

'I was actually being serious, Norva. It's not funny.'

'Do I look I like I'm laughing?'

She didn't. She wasn't.

There was a loud knock on the door.

Ringo barked excitedly in our faces. Norva covered his snout.

'Dial it back, baby,' she said to him. 'Who the hell is that now?' she said to me.

She kissed her teeth. 'Best thing about tower block life is the community. Worst thing about tower block life is the community.'

We went to the door together.

I looked through the peephole.

'It's Katie.' I sighed, relieved.

I unbolted and unlocked the door. As she stood in the frame, Ringo jumped on her, covering her black uniform in white fur. She gathered us into a hug.

'I'm sorry, I'm so sorry,' she said.

We hugged her tightly back. I didn't want to say it was OK, because it very much wasn't. She arrested Pap. We should hate her, really, but of course we didn't. She stepped back and wiped her eyes.

'I didn't want to arrest him, I didn't. Sharp – the Inspector – made me.'

'Yeah, we know,' Norva said.

'You do?' she replied.

'Yes,' said Norva, whispering theatrically. 'We know everything.'

'We also know you didn't want to do that,' I added. 'We heard.'

'I'm making such a mess of this case, I really am,' Katie groaned.

'You're doing your best,' I said, lying somewhat.

Katie looked at Norva. 'I love you both so much. How are you? You have food? You have money? You know what to do in an emergency? You remember Our Plan?'

We nodded. 'Yes, we'll survive,' I said.

'But Pap might not,' Norva muttered.

Katie looked into the flat behind us. 'Who's looking after you tonight? she asked.

Norva and I answered at the exact same time.

'Jane.'

'Serena.'

Katie narrowed her eyes.

'Which one is it?'

I stayed silent this time.

'Jane, it's Jane,' said Norva. 'She just messaged us to say come down.'

'Are you lying to me, Norva?'

'Never that, Kitty Kat,' Norva said.

'OK,' said Katie, cautiously appeased. 'Listen, this had to be a flying visit. I have to join Burnett and DCI Sharp at the station…' She looked at the floor. 'To continue the investigation. Now, I know you heard what she said…'

We nodded.

'…and I know you heard my reply.'

We nodded.

'Trust me when I say this. Again. I believe your Dad. 100%. We know he didn't do this.' She reached into her pocket. 'Look, here are my work numbers – mobile and desk. Text or call me. For anything. Whenever. I'll be back later.'

She kissed us both on the head, gave us the saddest of smiles and shut the front door behind her.

41

Norva leaned against the front door. 'Katie's not cut out for Police life, is she?' she said, drumming her fingers against her lips.

'How so?'

'Nik. Think about it. She just came up here, knowing exactly what kind of girls we are, and told us that the entire group of detectives assigned to this case are at the station. I love her, but it's all a bit basic, no?' She shook her head. 'Get your shoes on. The coast is clear.'

I tied the laces on my left trainer.

'Oh wait,' she said. 'We could do this the hard way – the 'fun' way – or you know, the easy way. Let me check.'

Norva ran down the hallway, and I tied the laces on my right trainer.

I heard her pulling and rummaging through drawers. Norva returned with the keys.

'Like I said, always in the kitchen!' she said, holding them near my face.

'Shouldn't the police have those keys? Wasn't Officer Burnett supposed to be setting up the Investigation Room?'

'Absolutely.'

She shut the door.

'I've been marking the timelines and waiting for my moment. That moment is now.'

She locked the door behind her.

We took the lift down to the lobby.

Norva tried the door to Pap's office. It was unlocked. The door swung open.

'Katie, Katie, Katie,' Norva said. 'Really? Even worse than I thought. Unless…'

'Unless what?'

'Unless she's intentionally being sloppy to help us out, leave loopholes for us to jump through?'

We looked at each other.

'Nah,' we said in unison.

Norva stepped back-first into the room.

'Ta da!' she said, smiling. 'I need your skills now, so get yourself behind his desk.'

I looked cautiously around the lobby and stepped in. The Murder Investigation Room – in its former guise as Pap's office, anyway – was probably my favourite place on The Tri.

Between the ages of five and ten, I used to pretend it was mission control and I could send the people of The Tri to space. His office contained:

- Ten CCTV screens
- Two desks
- Two old PCs
- Two chairs

Pap used to have a full-time assistant. A nice lady. Pamela Costner. Portuguese. Pretty. Plump. When she died, the council didn't replace her. Pap was on his own.

The police had taken their laptops, but left their photographs pinned to the wall. I acutely avoided looking at the image of Hugo's arm.

Instead I looked towards the corner of the room, where the cage-cabinet sat. It was locked. Nine 20 litre cans of paint stacked on top of each other.

I was so sick of that paint. I hated it.

I sat down.

'You ready for this, Nik?'

'Ready for what?'

'I need you to hack the mainframe.'

I looked at her quizzically. 'Hack the mainframe…?'

'You know, get in there,' she pointed at Pap's computer.

'You mean log in?'

'Sure, whatever – just open it up. Need intel. Get on it.'

I shook the mouse and the computer awoke; the dialogue box appeared on-screen. Pap's username was there, JA-02, but the password box remained empty.

I had no idea what it could be.

'Norva, I'm going to suggest some passwords, write them down so I don't retry them and waste time.'

'OK, ready. And Go!'

1111: The dialogue box shook.

JosephAlexander: The dialogue box shook.

NikNorva1113: The dialogue box shook.

'Awww, I'm sad that wasn't it,' said Norva.

JoeNorvNik1: The dialogue box shook.

'Look around the room,' I said. 'There might be a clue. If I try too many times, I'll lock it. I'm hoping it offers me a hint.'

Norva looked around the room, and at Pap's desk.

'What about Corner1222?' she suggested.

I tried it. The dialogue box shook.

'Hint?' appeared on the computer. Finally.

'Norva, we have a hint!' I clicked it.

Hint: FamMotto

'Oh my god, how basic can you get Pap? This is online Safety 101,' Norva said, rolling her eyes.

I typed *alexandersassemble* into the box and we were in.

Pap's computer opened up on his emails. A plethora.

'Goldmine!' whispered Norva, as she stood in the doorway.

At the top of the list, most recently received was an email from a Daniel Bartlett at the council.

Date: Tue 25/07 12:32
Subject: Apologies

Mr Alexander,

On behalf of the council today, I would like to extend an apology for the behaviour of Donald DeVos. His outburst and accusation does not reflect the views of the council, nor do we base our beliefs on reports on Cloud Nine news.

When the tragic matter at The Triangle is resolved, we will reschedule our hearing.

Best regards,
Daniel Bartlett, Head of Estates

'Donald DeVos sounds like a dork,' Norva said.

I nodded. 'But what was this hearing? What's Pap done?'

I looked at other emails from Daniel Bartlett.

Date: Fri 20/07 11:07
Subject: Hearing date

Mr Alexander,

Regarding the accusation(s) against you of misconduct due to unfair and unreasonable scheduling of repairs at The Triangle, and your formal warning, the council would like to invite you to a hearing with myself, Donald DeVos, Director of Estates, and Betsy Muller, Head of HR.

Please confirm your availability for Tuesday 25 July at 10:00. I do hope this time works; it is directly after First Aid training, which you are required to attend.

Best regards,
Daniel Bartlett, Head of Estates

I took a photo of the screen.

Printing was for old, patient people who enjoy noise and heartbreak.

'Pap was under investigation, Norva,' I said. 'The meeting with them was today. I'm going to look at other emails from Friday.'

I scrolled down the list.

An email thread between Mrs K and Pap. She was demanding repairs to her flat.

Pap had replied.

Date: Fri 20/07 13:08

Subject: Re: Repairs, when?

Thank you, again, for the many pierogis Mrs K, but I really cannot push you any further up the maintenance list. Not this time. I will discuss this with you this evening, following the meeting.

Joe.

I read the email to Norva.

'So, Pap was too scared to tell the whole truth to the police, because he was under investigation at work?' said Norva. 'Under investigation? For helping people? What are the council on?'

'Well, there are systems and waiting lists, Norva,' I said. 'You can't just flaunt the rules. But yes, it seems like an overreaction on their part. He was afraid of being fired, I suppose. He might have thought – probably rightly – that we'd have to move out too.'

'Good point,' said Norva. 'But murder is like a million times worse than painting an old lady's flat – why hasn't Kowalski just come clean?'

'I don't know.' I shrugged. It was very odd.

I took a photo of the screen.

There were other emails from Friday afternoon. From Jane. A long chain of emails. Back and forth. All day.

I clicked the first one.

Date: Fri 20/07 15:42
Subject: Re:re:re:re:re later

Hahahahaha! Yes, well, we have the same sized feet. That's a sign, love. Can't wait to get this meeting done and see you tonight. xoxoxoxoxoxoxo

'Gross! Delete! Un-see, undo, unsubscribe!' said Norva, clutching at her chest.

'It's not nice, but it's confirmation on their 'situation',' I said. 'And the shoes – same sized feet? She's using his shoes, but why? What's she doing?'

'She should buy her own shoes.' Norva kissed her teeth.

I took a photo of the screen.

There were other emails. Noise complaints. Lift out of order note for Corner Two. An unpaid bill notification. I scrolled forward, forward until I found what we were really looking for.

'Found it, Norv' I said. I clicked the chain open.

Date: Fri 20/07 23:05

Subject: Apology

Joseph,

Tonight was heated. I apologise for the way I behaved. You
and I are passionate people. I hope we can put this behind us
and move forward as friends and as a community.

HK-W

Date: Sat 21/07 00:31

Subject: Re: Apology

Hugo – it's me who needs to apologise. It was heated and I
was rude. We'll make this work! I'll make the flat look great in
the morning. If I don't see you, enjoy the market. Joe.

'So they had made up!' Norva shouted. 'This is
amazing! We out here cracking this case like pistachios.'

'It narrows the time of death window, from ten
thirty to eleven-o-five,' I replied.

I looked at the computer.

'It's brilliant, but we need more. Say Pap was the
murderer – he could have faked these emails. Somehow.'

Norva was silent.

'You're right, why you gotta pee on my chips like this?'

'I'm being…'

'Thorough. Yes I know,' she said glumly.

I took a photo of the screen.

42

I stood up.

'Erm, where you going?' Norva said from the doorway. 'You need to get into the CCTV. Access, please.'

I sat back down at the desk, not really knowing where to look. I clicked onto the council server. Achingly slow. The folders appeared one by one, by date last opened.

```
Invoices
Incidents
Accidents
Cameras
```

That last one was worth a try. Surely. Inside the folder sat subfolders for each Corner. Inside of those folders were video files for each camera for each day for the last seven days.

There were four folders for each camera in Corner one.

- The lift by the lobby
- Chute on First Avenue
- Chute on Second Avenue
- Chute on Third Avenue – where George, Hugo and Serena, and Jane live.

I was quietly impressed by the system and structure. I was unimpressed by the number of cameras.

'I actually found the files, Norva!' I exclaimed. 'We might actually be able to find something here.'

'Yeah, I know – why do you think I was stunting for the cameras?' she asked. 'I was assisting Future You with your hacking.'

'Where shall we start?

'Find the files for the lift. Start today, to see if it worked. We were at the lift around three this afternoon, right?'

'I'm not sure the files for today will be there yet,' I said, 'but let's have a look.'

I found a folder called C1_Lift. That folder contained files for the last five days. I clicked on the folder marked today and the most recent file at the top.

C1_Lift_2507_6

It opened to a black and white, frankly fuzzy video. But it was clearly Corner One. Clearly the lift.

Along the bottom, as if to prove itself, it read 'C1 Lift' and showed the time. 15:00.

The video had a total duration of three hours.

'Yes!' I turned to Norva. 'Seems like the video is automatically uploaded to this server every eight hours.'

I turned to the computer with a smile. 'This system is pretty decent,' I said impressed.

C1_Lift_2507_6 15:00

The Police and Katie appear.

I scrubbed through the video.

Norva and I appear.   I watched myself call the
the lift.

The lift opens and Norva looks directly at the
camera, at us. She sticks her tongue out, twists her
braids. I look annoyed.

'Ha, yas! There I am. We know this was today.
Friday night files, please.'

'OK!' I shouted, 'I can do this!'

Norva smiled at me. 'I know you can.'

I clicked back through the folders to Friday. The
most recent file at the top.

C1_Lift_2007_8

The time read 21:00.

I scrubbed through until 22:25. People poke the
lift button. They throw their hands up and walk away.

'That's right, the lift was broken,' I muttered
under my breath. 'And not fixed until Monday morning,'
added Norva.

C1_Lift_2007_8 22:32

Pap arrives at the lift. He jabs furiously at the button, looks up and down at its doors. He kicks at them. He turns around.

Jane arrives. She puts a hand on his shoulder and tries to hold his hand.

'Leave it out, Jane!' Norva shouted.

They wait. They have a conversation. It's heated. Arms flailing. Gesticulations.

Pap heads towards the staircase. Jane walks towards The Hub.

C1_Lift_2007_8 22:35

Hugo and Serena wait by the lift. Hugo is unsteady. He stumbles.

'He looks rough,' Norva said.

'Heatstroke?' I reply.

Hugo leans against the wall. He is waving his arms around, animatedly. Serena puts her arm around him and gently touches his curls.

Barry walks to the lift, points to it.

Hugo and Serena walk to the staircase. Barry walks towards The Hub.

I rewound the videos quickly and filmed them on my phone.

'OK, time to switch it up,' Norva said. 'Corner One, Third Avenue, Friday night. I want to see if Hugo made it home.'

C1_3AVE_2007_8

I scrubbed through the file until 22:50. The camera was positioned at the middle of the Avenue, pointing at the Chute.

C1_3AVE_2007_8 22:50

The doorway to the stairwell opens. Serena emerges first. She's holding Hugo's hand. He leans over the Avenue, next to the Chute. They look down, over The Tri. Her hand on his back.

'He's catching his breath,' I said.

'I'm not surprised,' said Norva. 'Walking 20 flights of stairs when you feel off is not the one.'

Hugo and Serena disappear off camera.

'Alright,' said Norva. 'Saturday morning from twelve fifteen. Let's see it.'

I held my breath.

I started the video at 00:10. Just in case.

No movement. I scrubbed through to 00:15.

The back of someone appears.

'Norva look!'

A person wearing black is dragging a very large Tri bag behind them. They open the chute, squat down, slowly lift the bag and push it into the chute.

They disappear down the stairs.

'Oh my god, who is that? That must be Hugo in the bag!' Norva said.

I rewound the video and filmed the screen. The CCTV played on.

'I think this is it,' I said to Norva. I turned to her. 'I think we've got it.'

She stared at the screen.

'What do we do now?' I asked.

'You got the footage, right. Let's bounce and look at it in more detail.'

I looked back at the screen. 00:17

'Norva, wait! There's someone else!'

I scrubbed back. Phone ready to record.

C1_3AVE_2007_8 22:17

A person wearing black stands at the chute. They're holding a very large Tri bag in one hand and Tri paint can in the other. They open the chute.

The person throws the paint can into the chute. They squat down and lift the bag into the chute. They walk up the avenue, towards the flats. They change their mind and turn around, disappearing down the stairs.

I sat back in the chair. Confused.

'Hugo's in one of those bags Nik, but which one?' Norva said. 'And Pap is one of those people, but which one? Nobody's limping?'

The lift doors opened in the lobby.

'Holy moly, someone's coming!' Norva hissed. 'Oh my god, oh my god! Quick! Move!'

I immediately froze on the spot.

'That's the opposite of moving!' Norva shouted.

I reached over and turned the PC off without shutting it down, silently begging for mercy from the computer gods for my sin. I patted myself down, checking I had my phone and the lid. I did.

I leapt out of the room as Officer Burnett walked in. I stood panting at the door.

'What the hell's going on here? What's not moving?' His voice rose, 'Why are you in the Investigation Room? This is a crime!' He shouted. 'You are trespassing!'

He reached for his radio.

'Officer Smyth, come in. Over,' he shouted to his handset. 'Officer Smyth, you've compromised the Investigation Room. Your pets are in here. Over.'

The handset buzzed, but no reply.

'Officer, officer, officer,' Norva said. 'We didn't realise this was your – what did you say? – Investigation Room? This is just our dad's office!'

'Girlie,' Officer Burnett said slowly. 'Don't play with me. I know you're not stupid. Look at the walls.'

I couldn't look at them again. I didn't want to see.

'Ah, I see. I'm sorry,' Norva said, looking around the room. 'It's a really great spot for a room like this,' she said, her words Splenda sweet. 'Why did you choose it? You set it up on Monday – when Katie, I mean, Officer Smyth – arrived. Didn't you? Right, Nik?'

She spun around to face me.

I nodded.

Officer Burnett shifted on the spot.

'It made sense at the time.'

'Made sense? An investigation room with sensitive information, in a place where many people – potential suspects included – walk past? Regularly? I suppose so.'

'Well, DCI Sharp signed it off so…'

'Made sense in a room that has multiple sets of keys?'

He looked at the floor.

'I didn't know you had access! I assumed I secured all the keys. I accounted for them all with, with…' His voice trailed away.

'With the caretaker, your prime suspect, our dad?' asked Norva. 'Ah, this is a bit of a pickle isn't it? My fault! I should have just known to give them to you. Somehow. Obviously,' Norva said. 'Yes, as soon as DCI Sharp returns, I'll apologise to her, personally, and let her know about my mistake. My lack of oversight.'

Norva smiled at him.

'No, no,' he protested. 'You don't have to do that,' he coughed. 'No need, no need…'

Officer Burnett's radio crackled into life.

'Officer Burnett, this is Officer Smyth,' sighed a weary Katie. 'How can I assist? Over.'

We stared at him. He stared back.

'Situation all resolved, Officer Smyth. My mistake. Out.'

43

'Had to throw Katie a bone there. She needs to catch a break, don't you think?'

'Definitely.'

I called for the lift and the doors rumbled open. Norva stepped in. She was grinning.

'Anyway, distraction over, and – Praise Beyoncé – the lift is right here, because I'm gonna burst! Receipt review. Right. Now. Because – Oh My Days.' She clapped her hands. 'We've got a bumper crop of evidence here, and it's time to harvest. Get. That. Doc. Open. Show me. Show me!'

She rubbed her hands together in glee.

'OK,' I exhaled. 'Let's do this. Let's start with Hugo.'

'And Go!' Norva said, pressing the button marked 22. The lift rose from the ground.

'We know Hugo was alive at five past eleven, because he sent Pap an email then,' I said. 'Assuming that he sent it, that is.'

'Yep – and we have to assume, for now,' Norva added. 'Hugo is definitely in one of those black bags we saw going into the chute at twelve fifteen – or – twelve seventeen. Both bags looked hench!'

'Let's think about this. Let's use facts and evidence to deduce.'

Norva rolled her eyes.

'We know how heavy and awkward the fake body—'

'Hugo Too,' Norva interjected.

'—the fake body was yesterday,' I continued. 'There's just no way you could carry a body and a paint can at the same time.' I shook my head. 'No chance.'

'Yeah, you right. Unless you're like Superman or something.' She turned to me. 'Superman's definitely not real, right?'

'Even if he was, he wouldn't have a motive for this case, Norva.'

Norva nodded. 'So this means, whoever the first person was, at twelve fifteen, was the person carrying the body. They're the murderer.'

'And the person at twelve seventeen...' Norva began.

I reached for my phone and played the video. Norva leaned on my shoulder to look.

'Person Twelve Seventeen was carrying a Tri Paint can – see, there. Pap says only he has access to them. So Person Twelve Seventeen... '

'Is Pap! He didn't do it?' Norva shouted. 'He didn't do it! He didn't do it,' she sang.

'Also, look, Norva,' I said. 'Twelve Seventeen also walks towards the flats and then turns back.'

'Maybe he was going to see Jane, and thought, 'you know what, nah, it's too late. Don't need the aggro'.'

'Exactly,' I said excitedly.

Norva squeezed me tight.

'We've flipping done it, haven't we?' She screamed. She jumped up and down in the lift. It shook and moaned under the extra stress.

'Stop jumping, Norva. We haven't 'done it' yet. Back to the facts. This puts the time of death officially between five past eleven and twelve fifteen, but taking our re-enactment into account – you need time to wrap the body – I'd say the deed was complete by five past twelve at best.' I shrugged at Norva. 'What do you think?

'Sounds legit,' Norva smiled at me. The smile quickly faded. 'But that means Mark is twelve fifteen, doesn't it Nik?' She sighed. 'I can't believe this. Such a disappointment – to put it mildly.'

The lift stopped and the doors opened slowly revealing Mrs Kowalski.

'Perfect! Let see how this plays out,' Norva whispered.

44

Mrs Kowalski wasn't carrying anything around her wrist, for once. It was strange to see her unburdened and unadorned.

She watched us step out of the lift but didn't step in. Instead, Mrs K stood next to us.

'Girls, I heard about your Papa!' she said, panicked. 'I tried to find you, feed you, and confess.'

'We're not hungry,' I said.

'Speak for yourself,' said Norva. 'We're the best we can be right now, Mrs K, you?'

Mrs K looked at floor. 'I don't feel so good. I made things worse.'

'How so?' I asked.

Let's hear it. From the horse's mouth.

'I didn't tell the truth, and now there's more trouble.' Her upper lip was moist. She licked the sweat away. I turned away with a grimace.

'More trouble?' Norva asked innocently.

'Yes, I kept secrets.'

'Which ones?' I asked.

'Secrets about everything. About your Papa. Where he goes at night. He's been naughty.'

'You mean with Jane?' Norva said flatly. 'We know about that.'

'Oh no, that not secret,' she said. 'Everyone knows that.'

I looked at Norva.

'They do?' I mouthed.

Norva gagged and shrugged.

'I mean on Friday night,' Mrs K said.

'Weren't you with your friend? Working on your project?' asked Norva.

'Yes,' she said.

'Is Pap your 'friend'?' I asked.

'Yes!' she said, louder.

'Is Pap stepping out on Jane with you?' asked Norva.

'Norva, that's gross.'

'Why gross?' Mrs Kowalski said. 'I'm old, not

dead! But no, he helped me with my project, but I didn't tell Police.'

'Why though?' I said.

'He said keep quiet, or he'd get fired. So I did. I said nothing. But I hate the Police,' she spat. 'Not on our side. When we arrived in North London, 1968, they beat up Mr K. Bad. Broken eye, broken nose, broken leg.'

I shuddered. 'I'm sorry to hear that.'

'And now they're doing it again,' she continued. 'I kept quiet. But this time, I should have talked. That Sharp came to me, and asked "what do you know?" I told her nothing. Then I see your Papa arrested! I need to fix things! I'm sorry, girls!'

'You can fix it now,' Norva said. 'Will you?'

Mrs K nodded.

I reached for my phone. 'Tell us your truth, Mrs Kowalski,' said Norva.

I put my phone in front of us.

'Angle the phone better please. I look like a ghoul,' she said.

Mrs K reached into her pocket and took out a dusty, dry lipstick and smeared it around the vicinity of her mouth. Mostly on her teeth. She took a deep breath and looked into the camera.

'Recording?' she said.

I nodded.

She took a deep breath.

'Joseph Alexander was with me, Ksenia Kowalksi, on Friday night. He was repairing my flat. Number two two two. He left just after twelve fifteen. I know the time because I take my teeth out at that time. He took big bag of rubble, old wallpaper, old clothes and a paint can to the chute. He will get in trouble for helping me; the Council don't like it. But he's not a murderer. Not Joe.'

I put the phone away.

Norva hugged Mrs Kowalski tight.

'You're legendary, Mrs K. A true icon. Take care, OK?'

'Yes, yes girls. I will,' she said with a wave of her hand. 'Be safe now. There's still a murderer on the loose.'

I shuddered and looked over at Norva. 'We know,' I said sullenly.

'Stay with me tonight?'

We shook our heads. 'We're crashing at George's.' Norva said.

Mrs Kowalski went to walk away.

'Hang on Mrs K, what was your project?' I asked.

Mrs K sighed. 'It's been four years since I lost my husband. Four years. Before he die, he made me promise…'

She put on an old man's voice, '…Promise me! Promise me you will fix the spare room and make art again. Promise! I promised him and I didn't do it. Room stayed messy for three and a half years. When it started to get warm, I knew it was time to fix it. I can't go on another year. I wanted it ready for Mr K's anniversary. And now it is. Bye girls. Keep me in loop?'

'Of course,' I said quietly.

She walked into her flat.

'Wow,' said Norva, rubbing her eyes. 'Just. Wow. There's Pap's alibi.'

We hugged each other. Tightly.

'I told you he didn't do it', said Norva.

'And I told you we needed the evidence to prove it,' I retorted with a smile.

We held hands.

'Before we do anything else, get that video into the world. Upload that baby now.'

I did, straight to YouTube. I copied the link into a new message. I attached photos of the emails to it and sent it to Katie.

'Pap's going to be free,' I said with a wide smile. 'I'm so happy!' I sighed.

'Don't be too sprung, yet,' Norva said in a low voice. 'We know this already, but Mrs K is right about a murderer on the loose. And we don't know how they did it.'

My smile dimmed.

'What do you mean, Norva?'

'Think about it.'

I wracked my brain. Think, Nik. Think. I thought back to the video. The timings. The paint can.

Weapon: Paint can

'Norva!' I whispered. 'If Mark was Mr Twelve Fifteen, then Hugo was already in the chute when Pap got there. He put the paint can in first, directly on top of Hugo. The paint can is not the murder weapon, is it?'

Norva nodded.

'Way ahead of you.'

'So how did he die, Norva?'

45

Norva put her key in our front door. It swung open easily. Someone was in our flat.

Again.

The hallway was dim. The sun had started to set. I held my breath, and reached for Norva's hand. My heart beat visibly through my t-shirt. At least I thought it did.

'Stay back,' she whispered. 'I got you.'

'Hello?' Norva called out. 'Who the flip is here now?'

'Me, girls!' called a voice from the lounge.

Jane. Again.

We sighed. 5% relief.

We looked at each other.

'What do you want?' Norva called out. 'Why do you have to do this creeping in the shadows thing?' she shouted.

'Oh, I'm sorry!' She said, 'I just want to talk.'

A light flicked on in the distance.

We inched down the hallway, slowly. Short steps. Jane sat silently on the sofa. Ringo, the traitor, was curled in her lap. She stroked him gently and she stared ahead. We stood still.

I squeezed Norva's hand.

'Hello girls,' Jane said quietly. A tear ran down her face.

'How did you get in?' Norva asked.

'It was unlocked,' she replied.

Lies.

'Was it, Jane? I know I locked it. Especially with Pap being…away.'

'I knew you didn't go to Serena's,' she said. 'I was…worried about you.'

'If you're worried about us, why are you sitting here in the dark?' I interjected. 'It's not helping.'

'Yeah, we know you have a key,' Norva sneered.

'Y-you do?' said Jane, clearly taken back.

'Of course, how else would you get in? Your gaslighting doesn't work on us,' Norva said.

'Gaslighting?'

'Yeah, it's when you make people think they're going crazy, on purpose, when they're not.'

Jane cried, 'Oh my word, I'm not trying to make you think that! There's just something I have to tell you. It's really important, and I didn't want to do it. Not this way.'

More tears. Sobs, actually.

'What is it?' Norva replied. 'That you're checking our dad? Jane, we been knew.'

Jane turned around sharply on the sofa.

Ringo fell off her lap and onto the floor.

'You *know*!?' she said loudly, now staring at us. She wiped her eyes, vigorously. 'You already know!? I came to tell you, so you'd understand my behaviour over the last few hours.'

'Oh yeah, we know all about it,' said Norva. 'We've seen your emails.'

'You've read our emails? All of them? Please, no!'

Her eyes widened and her face went a deep red. She put her head in her hands.

'This is not how I wanted this to play out. At all.'

'So what's the deal?' asked Norva. 'How long has this,' she waved her hand around Jane, 'been going on?'

'About a year now,' she said, looking at her hands.

'*A YEAR!*' We shouted in unison.

We stared at each other.

How did we not see this? What kind of detectives were we? Who were we? What was life?

I questioned the core of our very existence.

'We were very discreet. Very discreet. We didn't want to upset you.'

'Have you...' Norva shuddered. '...been in this house?' she asked.

'Been in your house? I'm right here...'

Norva raised her eyes at her.

'Oh no!' shouted Jane, getting Norva's point. 'I've never stayed here. Ever. No, no, no.'

Norva relaxed. A little.

'Are you mad with me?' Jane asked pitifully.

'I'm pretty disgusted, yeah,' said Norva.

I nodded my head in agreement. 'It's not great,' I said.

'I mean, it's so disgusting. So gross. It's too much.' Norva went in. 'And we don't trust you. At all.'

'I understand,' she said. Jane reached for her bag.

'But really, right now,' Norva said, speaking softly, 'this is the least of our worries. We have bigger fish to fry. We all have. That is, as long as you don't try to pull any ridiculous stepmum business on us. OK?'

263

'Yes,' I added. 'Not now. Frankly, ever. Our energy needs to be focused on Pap. Not you.'

Jane nodded, and wiped her face. 'OK, girls. That's wonderful. Your generous spirits and overall maturity is exceptional. You are a real credit to your dad.'

Norva waved her hand, 'Yeah yeah yeah.'

She let go of my hand and walked to the sofa, sitting down firmly next to Jane.

'Now you've let yourself into our house, and told us your truth, we're free to ask you some questions. Deal?'

'Deal.'

46

Norva waved me over, and we squeezed together on the sofa. Jane in the middle. Ringo relegated to the floor.

'I'll start with an easy one,' Norva said 'Our keys. Did you get them from Pap?'

Jane looked down and nodded.

'How long have you had them?' I asked.

'A while.'

Norva leaned over to look and me. She shook her head and tutted.

'I'll go,' I said. 'Another easy one.' I was feeling brave. 'You were waiting for him on Friday night?

'Yes,' she leaned forward and put her head in her hands. 'I'm so scared, girls. I know that a lot of people were − and still are − talking about him. I don't want everyone in our business, but I can't even offer him an alibi for Friday night. It feels awful.'

'He doesn't need it,' I said. 'We figured it out.'

'What do you mean?' Jane said loudly. Her head spun between Norva and me.

'He was helping a neighbour, and when he finished, he came home,' I said. 'He was actually thinking about going to see you but he changed his mind.

'How do you know this?' she asked, shocked. She sat up straight. 'Is this true?' She looked at Norva.

Norva nodded slowly. 'No lies. I know you're shook. I get it, but we're not going to reveal our sources. Not yet anyway. So don't press us.'

'Did he not offer an explanation at all though? Not over the weekend, or on Monday?' I asked.

Jane shook her head. 'That's the thing. I couldn't get a clear answer. Said he had to do some cleaning up. That's how he got the limp.'

'He mustn't trust you that much, yet,' said Norva, a smile dancing on her lips.

Jane looked crestfallen. 'Maybe. Will you tell me which neighbour? Who was it?'

We shook our heads.

'Something's been definitely going on with him recently. All of this was great for a while – the sneaking around. It was fun. Thrilling…'

I looked over at Norva who was clearly dying on the inside.

'…but lately he's been more and more distant. Maybe he's not that into me anymore, that was why he didn't want to go public.' Jane sighed. 'Look, tell me straight – was he with Serena? I just know she's into him. Do you think he likes her? I think he likes her.'

'Like, 'like' likes her?' said Norva. 'What makes you say that?'

Jane sat back and rolled her eyes. 'I don't know. Maybe I'm just insecure, but she's always touching him, and being so friendly, and I know she doesn't like me.'

'Hmmm,' said Norva. 'Maybe so.' She turned to me. 'They'd make a cute couple though, wouldn't they? Serena and Pap?'

Norva looked at Jane. Jane looked sadly at the floor.

I shook my head.

'Not as cute as me and Mark though,' said Norva. 'We're goals.'

Jane looked up at her. 'Mark? No no, Norva. He means well, but he's…'

Ding! Ding!

My phone. I sat up and pulled it from my shorts. Norva looked expectantly at me.

'Is it Katie?'

I hoped it was. It wasn't.

Summer calls for new sandals! You deserve them. Treat yo self, girl! Find your local store here.

'Not her,' I said.

I showed the message to Jane. 'Sandal sale, Jane? Interested?'

'Not really,' she said, looking at Norva.

Norva looked at me, confused.

'It's just that you seem to be taking shoes that don't belong to you?'

Norva caught my drift.

'Yeah! And making a mess with them too!'

Jane looked perplexed. Then, clarity.

'You know about the boots? Ah!' she exclaimed, coming to a further realisation. 'So you were taking photos in my kitchen? You were investigating me?'

We stared at her until she spoke.

'OK, OK, yes, yes. I borrowed his spare pair of

boots, this morning. We have the same sized feet you know?' she said brightly.

Norva narrowed her eyes. 'Yeah, we know.'

Jane looked at her quizzically, until she realised how she knew. She coughed in embarrassment.

'Oh yes, the emails. OK. I borrowed his boots this morning. There was a little spot in my kitchen wall that was fading. I wanted to cover it. Tiny job.'

'That's why it smelled of paint in there today?' I asked.

'Yes!' she said. 'Joe poured a bit of paint out for me after he came back from his meeting. He said he didn't care about the list any more. I could have some. Flip it. I did the job myself. Badly. I dropped the paint all over his shoes. I went to throw the paint away and clean the boots, but of course the chute is a crime scene. I walked all over the Avenue in a flap.'

'So the footprints all over the Avenue are yours?'

'Yes. Yes, they are.'

This was a comfort. Pap's not messy. He would never.

~~To-do: Pap's bootprints on Third Avenue~~

'I was speaking to him about it before he was…
taken away. He was urging me to tell DCI Sharp in case
she thought he was trying to obstruct justice or muddy
the waters…'

'Mission accomplished,' said Norva. 'Great job.'

Ding! Ding!

I reached for my phone. Katie? But it wasn't my
phone. It was Norva's.

'It's George. Says he's popping to Better Buy,
then we should come down for dinner. Let's meet him at
the shop. Maybe we'll see Mark.'

I stood up.

Jane reached for her bag again.

'Look, Jane,' Norva said, standing up. 'We're off.
Stay if you want. I think we can trust you. A tiny bit.'

Jane looked at me. I nodded.

'Don't be too liberal with that key though,' said
Norva. 'You're not family. And you never will be.'

47

'Why hasn't Katie replied to my message yet?' I whined. I called the lift. 'And why isn't Pap home yet?'

'It's not as simple as that,' Norva said. 'It's not just like, bloop, your girls handed over the receipts, off you pop, Pap. Freedom. There are procedures. You know how it goes. Facts and evidence.'

Norva stepped back. 'What is this timeline?' she whispered. 'I sound like you, and you sound like me!'

I smiled. 'A little bit.'

'It's like that thing about dogs and their owners, isn't it?'

'I'm not your dog, Norva.'

The lift arrived. No George.

'He must have left already – let's see if we can twist his arm into buying us some crisps or something, yeah?'

The lift door closed.

'This lift is our true office, innit?' said Norva. 'Miss Alexander, please recap.'

'OK, so Jane's out.'

Norva nodded. 'She didn't do it; she can't even paint her kitchen without the whole Avenue knowing about it. Indiscreet.'

'That just leaves Mark,' I said. 'Serena's received that note – she's devastated.'

Norva took a sharp intake of breath. 'Mark,' she sighed. 'Why do I still care about you like that?' She looked up at the roof of the lift. 'We'd better recap and piece it together, then.'

'Reviewing the CCTV and considering our experiment, it's clear that Hugo died in his flat. He wasn't brought up the stairs, he wasn't carried anywhere.'

'Agree,' she said. 'So what was Mark doing there? How did he get in?'

'To be confirmed. Our next priority. Also the paint can is out. We need a new method pretty quickly.'

'Definitely. Let's review the video of Hugo at the Hub later.'

'The motive is money. From this clock of Hugo's. Jane said he was coming into money, so did Timothy at the market earlier.'

'Also that clock scribble on his calendar?' Norva added.

'Yes,' I said. 'We need to find out which clock it is and find it! I should know more about it, I need time to think!' I said, exasperated.

'Serena's note co-signs all of that,' said Norva. All signs are really pointing at my boy, aren't they?'

I nodded.

'It doesn't look good, Norva,' I replied. 'We know he's broke – working with Pap whenever he can. He was at Serena's on Monday afternoon. She said he's been loitering. We've seen them walking across the Tri. Jane's unimpressed...'

'Not that I'll take her word for anything, but Serena and Mark were talking real close when Hugo's body was discovered. You know, officially, by the police.'

'What if Mark is blackmailing Serena?' I suggested. 'I think he wrote that note. Is that possible?'

'Anything is possible,' Norva said sadly.

'It makes sense, Norva,' I said. 'Also – Pap being away also helps him get more work here on The Tri, potentially. These motives are layered.'

I looked into Norva's eyes.

'We need to help Serena, Norva. We need to protect her. And keep Mark away. For all of our sakes.'

George was waiting for us in the lobby.

'Ayo, NSquared!' he said. 'You alright? What's the latest with Big Joe?'

'He didn't do it,' I said. We found the evidence, and sent it over to Katie.'

'Oh, word? You done did it already? I bow down. When's he getting home?'

'We don't know yet,' I said.

'These things take time, you know George, it's not an instant thing, like bloop, here are the receipts…'

Norva smiled at me.

'Aye, I don't know how the Police roll. I hope to never know, feel me?'

'George,' Norva said solemnly. 'In other news, we've got personal, family information to share. Goes no further though, OK?'

We did?

'Hit me, ladies. I ain't telling a soul.'

Norva took a deep breath, and shut her eyes.

'Pap's checking Jane,' she said.

She opened her left eye to check his reaction.

George closed his eyes and roared with laughter. When he opened them, he said, 'Yeah, obviously.'

So he knew too?

'That's the oldest of news. You being serious? You didn't know?'

He laughed. 'You two so busy spying on everyone else, you didn't think to look around your own house. Wack!'

'Alright, George, we get it – you can stop creasing up,' Norva said, kissing her teeth.

'OK OK OK, I'll allow it, I'll allow it.' He wiped tears from his eyes. 'You two bust me up, I'm just saying.' We walked to Better Buy. 'I can't wait for Big Joe to get back, rub it in all these haters' faces,' George said. 'You know everyone thinks he did it?'

'Yes, thanks for the reminder, George,' I said.

'Alright Sarky-snark, dial it back. You know I don't think he did it. Big Joe A is legit. No murderer. Definitely not. Nah, I reckon this was someone playing a long game. Someone with some real, deep reasons.'

48

'Let me fetch this ghee and English mustard for my mum real quick.'

We stood at the entrance of Better Buy in the dark.

'You not coming in?' George said.

'We'll wait here, thanks,' said Norva sharply. 'Sissy ain't in our good books right now.'

George shrugged. 'End all beefs!' he shouted as he disappeared into the shop.

Norva shouted after him, 'Get me some crisps, yeah?'

I chimed in, 'Oh and can I have a Vitonica?'

'A Vitonica!? He shouted back. 'You know how much that juice costs up in here?'

Sissy leaned past her fan and waved weakly at

us. Norva turned her back. I raised my head at her in acknowledgement. I had no choice; she trapped me.

Hugo's van was still parked in front of Better Buy. An old, long, dirty white van with wheels that desperately needed air. No cordon. No Officers. No movement since the investigation began.

Norva approached his van.

She wrote 'RIP Hugo N^2' with her finger in the grime on the driver's door.

I looked at her sternly.

She drew a heart around her scrawl, and looked at me with big eyes. 'Better?' she said.

'5% improvement,' I replied.

'Can't believe this van is still here,' said Norva. 'This investigation is a shocker.'

We peered through the windscreen.

She reached for her phone and turned on its flashlight. Scrunched up food wrappers, a magazine, and a book called an A-Z sat on the dashboard. 'Paper Citymapper,' said Norva.

A faded, once scented − I presumed − tree decoration hung from the rear view mirror. A red piece of fabric woven with gold threads was thrown on the passenger seat. I reached for my phone and took a photograph.

We looked through the windows at the back of the van. Disorder. Chaos. The van looked ransacked. On top of the piles of open, awkwardly-stacked boxes were more food wrappers. At least fifteen scrunched up balls of grease.

That was different.

I reached for my phone and scrolled back through my photographs.

'Look, Norva,' I said. 'These boxes weren't in there yesterday. What's going on? Those wrappers. Do you think Mark's been here? He's a burger eater. Serena doesn't strike me as a fast food fiend. Are these the ones in her flat?'

Norva wasn't listening.

'Things are alive in there, gross,' she said.

'What do you mean?' I asked, as I completed a final count of the wrappers.

'Look closely?' she said.

I put my face closer to the window.

She was right. There were flies. Everywhere. They existed on various points of the circle of life. Dead and alive.

I hadn't noticed on first glance. They seemed to be attracted to a large shallow box.

A box filled with rotten and rotting fruit.

Five dirty blenders.

'Why is Serena's stuff in there?' asked Norva. 'She said didn't have the keys to the van?'

'Maybe Mark does? Serena also said she only had one blender, too. These ones must be broken. Her operation is bigger than we thought!'

As I raised my phone to take a photo, a bright voice called out behind us in the dark.

'Hi girls!' Serena trilled cheerfully.

We immediately stepped away from the van. George stood next to her, laughing and swinging a thin blue plastic bag. Very neighbourly.

'Have you *seen* the state of the van? An absolute war zone.' Serena giggled. 'Fruit flies multiplying everywhere.'

'Dying everywhere too,' said Norva.

'Yes,' she said. 'Mark found the keys after you left, so I'm getting rid of some bits. Good job too. I had to declutter, streamline and minimise, darlings. Negative energy, you know?'

George dipped into his bag and threw Norva a small bag of crisps and handed me a Vitonica.

'That's on Serena,' he said. 'Not me, girl'

'Thanks so much!' I said excitedly. I quickly unscrewed the bottle and tipped the juice into my throat.

I didn't stop to sip.

'Chug! Chug! Chug!' Norva laughed, as the juice refreshed me, brought me back to life.

George shook his head. 'Girl, you wild. You need to slow down on that sugar roll,' he said.

'It will make you sick.'

49

'Oh, I'm so glad you're staying with Georgie tonight,' Serena said, clapping her hands together. 'I think it's good for you all to be together. Keep your spirits up!'

The lift felt way too small with four people in there.

'You're kipping?' asked George 'I…'

Norva slyly kicked him in the ankle to quiet him.

'Yay, pals together!' Norva replied cheerfully, linking arms with George. 'Jane's not as much fun as our boy.'

'Yeah, I agree with that,' Serena said with a laugh. 'I'm not entirely sure about her.'

I looked over at Norva.

'Not sure about Jane?' Norva asked. 'In what way?'

'Ah, I just don't think she's all that creative when it comes to fundraising. She could really make that money work harder, invest it, maximise the profits.'

'Do you invest, Serena?' I asked

'Yes, do you maximise your profits from Vitonica, dog walking and Yoga classes?' asked Norva, a hint of sarcasm in her voice.

Serena looked Norva straight in the eye. 'I don't.' She softened. 'But if I did have access to the money Jane has, I would be a whole lot better off – The Tri would be a whole lot richer. She's just a bit too worthy and charitable.'

'Maybe that's what Hugo saw in Jane?'

'Hugo and Jane?' George began to laugh.

Norva kicked him in the ankle to quiet him.

Harder this time.

Serena eyed him. She laughed. 'Yeah, I might have been wrong about that.'

'Couldn't be more wrong,' George said with a snort.

Ding! Ding!

My phone vibrated in my pocket.

'Is it?' Norva asked tensely.

A message from Katie.

Got it. On it. Stay safe – and out of the investigation room!

I nodded. Norva squealed with delight.

I smiled back and pushed the phone back into my pocket, next to the lid.

'Yo!' said George, 'Is that what I think that is? Big Joe back on the loose? Back in the game?'

Norva forcefully kicked him in the ankle to quiet him.

'What?' asked Serena, her voiced raised. 'Joe's being released? That's brilliant! I just knew he was innocent!'

The lift door opened onto Third Avenue, and we walked towards George's flat.

Serena's door opened and Mark stepped out.

Norva and I quickly reached for each other's hands.

'Serena…' I began quietly.

Mark looked surprised to see us. He stepped back into Serena's doorway.

'Hi Mark!' said Serena brightly, cutting me off. 'All done in the flat?'

Mark looked at Serena. His mouth hung open, his eyes narrowed in our direction. He nodded.

She turned to us.

'Mark's been helping me with Hugo's things. He's just darling, isn't he? So funny, really cheering me up, aren't you?'

Serena held his arm, tightly, smiling. Mark looked away.

'He's alright,' Norva said through tight teeth. 'I hope you find what you're looking for, Mark,' she said, looking him up and down, shooting a look at Serena.

Mark looked directly at the floor.

Uncomfortable and nervous.

He seemed desperate to get away.

Norva's eyes were fixed on Mark. But that's not unusual. They always were when he was around.

'I'll just go grab those bits for you, Serena, I'll be back,' said Mark, twisting his arm free from her grip.

'Serena,' I said quietly as Mark disappeared into the stairwell, 'please be carefully around him.'

'What do you mean?' she said, her smile dimming.

'I think he has...'

The front door next to us opened.

'I thought I could hear you!' Nina said brightly. 'Come in, dinner's ready.'

'Yes Mum!' said George, pushing us into his flat.

I looked back at Serena, who stood fixed to the spot, looking into space.

50

Nina had put on a spread.

'Check it out,' said George. 'Bare eats for the Alexander sisters!'

We sat down to samosas, pakoras, jalebi. It was incredible.

'You know how this cooking game goes, that's for sure, Ms Khan,' said Norva between bursting mouthfuls.

'This is beyond delicious. A chef's kiss to you!' Norva kissed her fingers.

'Thank you,' I said. 'It's really lovely. And very kind of you.'

'My pleasure!' she said with a smile. It's what you need right now.'

It was. It really was.

After the feast, Norva threw herself on George's bed.

'George. Drink. Water. Now.'

'Alright, your highness. Nik, same?'

'Yes please.'

I looked around George's bedroom. I say bedroom, it was more of a recording studio. Or wanted to be, when it grew up.

A single bed pushed in the corner. A desk with two monitors, headphones, microphone. Adjacent to this desk, another table with a keyboard. George was actually dedicated to his craft. I was impressed. Maybe I would check out his Soundcloud after all.

Norva sat up, 'He did it, Nik. My waters, they're calling it. He's blackmailing her.'

'It's the most likely scenario,' I said.

'Serena clearly doesn't suspect he's the murderer − or blackmailer. You see the way she held his arm?'

I nodded.

'Is that how you behave when you're scared of someone?'

'It's not, no.'

'See the way Mark's just free ranging in her flat. He's there, she's not? Helping her with Hugo's things.'

Looking for the clock more like.

Norva lay back down. 'Men are such a disappointment,' she said.

'Not all men, thank you very much,' said George, walking back in the room with two glasses of water.

'Nah, you're included in that mix, mate,' she said, 'with your loose lips and flapping gums in the lift. We don't want anyone to know about Pap's release. It's too dangerous. Also, don't think I've forgotten about your backstage shenanigans with TrojKat.'

'Easy girl, take a sip of water.' He handed her a glass.

I changed the subject.

'You have a great room, George. Your equipment looks really interesting.'

'It is, Nik! It's nuts. Between this stuff, my phone and my talent, nothing's going to hold me back. I'm telling you. I'm gonna be large and in charge.'

Norva sat up, suddenly. 'Show us how it works,' she said.

George rubbed his hands together. He opened up his software and ensured the microphone was connected.

'Simple. Spit your bars in there.' He pointed to the microphone.

'It gets recorded in here,' he pointed to his computer.

As he talked, the audio waves oscillated wildly.

'Hello! Hello! Hello!' I said from across the room.

The lines on his screen bounced and wobbled. I was impressed. This was interesting – and potentially – very useful.

'How much storage do you have George?' I asked.

'I got loads. I'm stacked. Terabytes for everyone.'

'Keep recording overnight, yeah?' said Norva. 'I want to hear your snores. I think we can mix them into a fun track.' She slumped her shoulders and mimicked George. 'You know the Internet will love it, bro. Big on the Net.'

'Funny,' he replied. 'But yeah, actually I will, you know. That's a good idea, Norv.'

Norva took a bow.

As if on cue, we heard a huge explosion.

Then screams.

51

We ran out of George's bedroom, through his front door and onto Third Avenue. Plumes of black smoke rose from a fire below. We leaned over and craned our necks for a closer look.

Hugo's van was engulfed in flames. An inferno. It was difficult to see without our telescope but the windows were certainly smashed, and the back doors were open.

Incident! Hugo's van explodes Tue 24/07 21:32

People leaned out of their windows and gathered on the Avenues.

People rushed out of Bermuda's and Better Buy. They held their phones high in the air, capturing every single moment.

Sirens sounded in the distance.

'Norva!' I shouted, heart thumping. 'See if anyone is live streaming this. Quickly!'

Norva fumbled for her phone, but no need.

A small Serena ran towards Better Buy. She looked tiny, but her voice loomed large.

'That's all I had left! All I had left of his things!' she screamed hysterically.

'I thought you all liked me!? Really liked me!?'

Her voice echoed across The Tri.

'I thought we were family here? You're all fake. Fake! You won! I'm leaving, OK? You won! First my brother, now me!'

She sobbed.

My heart sunk for Serena.

Sissy wheeled over to her to offer a hug but Serena slapped her hands away.

Norva laughed. 'Sissy deserved that!'

The fire smelled like diesel obviously, but also of cooked fruit. Apple Crumble. It was almost pleasant.

'Where is he? Where is he? Where is he?' said Norva. Our eyes darted across The Tri.

'Who?' George asked excitedly. 'Who did it?'

We stayed silent.

'There.' I said, pointing.

Mark was in the gardens, next to The Rec. He leant against a cherry tree, breathing heavily. Like he'd just run away from something.

'Called it,' Norva said flatly. No emotion in her voice. She turned away from the Avenue.

'You think Mark is behind it all?' George exclaimed. 'Wow. *WOW*. That boy is basic! You sure?'

We stayed silent. Loose lips sink ships. Or you know, murder cases.

'Oh. My. Days,' George exclaimed, as we went back into his room. 'The Tri is WILD this week – and it's only Tuesday. Absolute savagery.' He shook his head. 'Is this real life?'

'It doesn't feel like it, does it?' I said.

Norva summoned me. 'Let's get out there.'

She leant over to George's microphone. She pushed it as close to the wall as she could against the wall between George's room, and Serena's flat.

'Keep that running. All night,' she whispered.

52

'Come on, come on!' Norva said, jabbing the button for the lift. 'This is ridiculous.'

'Everyone's going home after the explosion, what do you expect?' I said.

'I expect them to flipping walk!' She poked the button again. She kissed her teeth.

'That's what we should do!' I said, throwing up my hands. 'Let's just take the stairs – we're wasting time here.'

I pulled open the door to the stairwell.

Her shoulders dropped. 'Alright. Let's do it,' she said quietly.

We ran down the stairs. Two at a time.

On the eighteenth floor, we caught our breath. Norva put her arm out to stop me.

'Let me pause it up right here a sec,' she said.

'What's the plan, anyway?' I asked her between deep gulps of pee-tinged air. 'What are we going to do down there?'

I hunched over. Hands on my knees.

Norva leaned against the wall.

'It's time to level up. We're going to have to be strong, tell some proper lies and add a pinch of mayhem to figure this out.'

'We are?'

She nodded. 'Let's keep going.'

On the thirteenth floor, we heard footsteps. We slowed down our pace down to a creep. The smell of diesel wafted up.

We saw him before he saw us. The top of Mark's head appeared.

I held my breath.

Norva looked at me and nodded. I nodded in return.

We were ready. I gulped.

Mark stopped to catch his breath. He looked up. His eyes met ours. He cursed under his breath.

'OK, Mark?' I asked. Faux concern.

'Yeah, yeah fine,' he panted, walking towards us.

'Sure? You don't look fine,' said Norva.

'Ah, I just went on a quick run,' he said.

I looked him up and down.

'A run? In the dark? In jeans?' I looked at Mark.

'He's really dedicated to fitness,' said Norva, looking at me. She sniffed. 'You smell of diesel, Mark.' Her hand flew to her mouth. 'You didn't run too close to the explosion, did you?'

'Nah, nowhere near it,' he said. Eyes fixed to the floor. 'Didn't see it. Listen, I've got to go. Mum needs me.'

He pushed past us.

'Mark?' Norva called to him.

'Yeah?' he asked, exasperated. 'What?'

'You know that clock Serena is looking for?' she said.

I stared at her.

Mark stood completely still.

'Yeah?' he said, stepping back down the stairs towards us.

Mark stood on the step above Norva. His face close to hers. In another dimension, she would have loved this scenario.

'What do you know about it? Have you seen it?' he demanded in a low voice.

'Possibly. I think we saw it in The Hub earlier.'

No, we didn't. My heart raced and my palms sprung water.

'You serious?' he said in a low snarl.

Norva gulped. 'Yeah – yep. I swear down. Didn't we? Didn't we Nik?' She turned to me with a smile.

I nodded. 'Pretty sure of it,' I said.

Lie.

He smiled widely. 'Ace,' he said, relieved. 'Nice one!' He ran up the steps two at a time.

The Fire Brigade had done their work by the time we reached the van. White smoke rose from its charred chassis.

Officer Burnett was on the scene, a cordon in place around the van.

Too little, too late.

His eyes met ours. Norva stood to attention and saluted him. He shook his head and continued keeping watch.

'I was hoping Katie might be here – with Pap,' I said.

Norva nodded. 'Me too. Check your video. Has it gone viral?'

I took my phone from my pocket and checked.

Five views. One comment.

'Big Joe innocent!'

George.

'No,' I replied.

'Alright,' Norva said excitedly. 'Let's move.'

53

'Stakeout time,' said Norva. 'You ready?'

I nodded wearily. I wasn't. I was tired. But, if justice doesn't sleep, neither did I.

'You need to look alive,' she said. 'This could get really real.'

I leaned against the wall. I put my hands in my pockets. Phone. Lid. I had everything I needed.

'I'm fine, I'm on it,' I said.

The lights were out in The Hub. I peered through the narrow windows in the doors.

Norva pulled Pap's keys from the pocket of her dress.

'I swear I'm never giving these up. Never. Pap will have to prise them from my cold dead hands.'

'Let's hope that never happens.'

'Yeah me too, obviously.'

Norva unlocked the door and we stood at the edge of the room, our backs to the wall. Hugo's desk stood in front, the chair cupboard on our right.

We spoke in whispers.

'I laid the bait,' said Norva, eyes shining in the dark. 'Let's see if he takes it.'

She looked around the room.

'If he has any sense, he'll go through the desk first. Might even slice into the chair.'

I winced.

'I hope not – Hugo really loved that chair.'

'What did I say about collateral damage? If he does, we're going to have to let it go.'

'I just don't want it to be violent. It will be like someone killing Hugo all over again,' I said.

'Well not really, it's a chair. Let it go.'

I shrugged. 'Alright, fine.'

'Right, we're going to need a place to hide, yet see all the action.'

She looked over to the cupboard. 'Perfect, in there. Let's angle up the desk a bit better, make these front row seats pay!'

We took either end of the desk and tilted it towards the door. It scraped loudly across the floor.

'Bloody hell!' whispered Norva. 'Don't let it be over before it begins!'

She stood back, crouched down and made a frame with her thumbs and index fingers.

'Yeah, that looks good to me. To the cupboard!'

She pulled its double doors.

The cupboard was stacked high with chairs. It was cold in there, and slightly dusty. A spider scuttled across the floor.

'Our room for the night,' Norva said. I threw her a weary look.

'It will be worth it, I promise. We'll learn so much.'

We pushed the chairs back deeper in to the cupboard and sat on the floor.

'Yeah, I know. The irony isn't lost on me either. We'll get a better view down here.'

I reached for my phone. The light illuminated our faces.

'Dim your torch! And your screen!' Norva said, panicked. 'Do you want us to get caught?'

'But I can barely see it!' I said. 'I could be using this time to research the clock, and Mark's method,' I said.

'It will have to wait!' she said, slapping the phone out of my hand and onto the floor.

Footsteps.

I fumbled for my phone and held my breath. My heart thumped in my chest.

The door to The Hub swung open.

The smell of diesel filled the room.

'Maybe not that long,' Norva whispered.

We peered through the crack of the door.

54

Mark stood in the centre of The Hub. He hadn't changed his clothes, but had added a light jacket. He held a can of spray paint in his right hand.

He walked around the room in circles, then to the window and looked out across the dark Tri. He reached for his phone and typed out a message.

When he was finished, he sat in Hugo's chair. He liked how comfortable he was, jugding by his murmur of approval. He put the can of spray paint on the desk, sat back in the chair and looked towards the ceiling.

Mark wheeled himself to the centre of The Hub in Hugo's chair and pushed himself around in small circles. He laughed to himself.

Ding! Ding!

Mark had a message. He looked at his phone and shouted 'For flip sake!' angrily to the room. His voice echoed around The Hub.

He stood up and pushed the chair away. He paced back to the desk, blocking our view. He took off his jacket, leaving it in a heap in front of the cupboard. In our reach.

The ransacking of the room began. He tore into Hugo's desk, loudly pulling the drawer onto the floor. He panted as he rifled through its contents.

Norva inched forward to grab his jacket. Her fingers spidered across the floor. She grabbed the collar and pulled it towards her. It slipped through the door and into her arms.

Norva sniffed his jacket deeply. She could feel my eyes on her in the dark.

'It's complicated!' she hissed.

I snatched it from her hands, and checked the pockets.

'No!' shouted Mark behind us. Then, the sound of Hugo's desk being flipped over.

I flinched.

I pulled the contents out and placed them on the floor behind me. I turned my back to the door, and to Norva. I reached for my phone to illuminate the objects.

- Keys
- Wallet
- A small star-shaped silver brooch, with diamonds on the outside
- A little bottle of tablets

Beyond the doors, Mark shook his spray can. The lid clicked off, paint hissed out.

I quickly took a picture of the collection before me, and stuffed the items back into Mark's pocket. I turned back to Norva, who was watching Mark spray paint against the wall. Against Barry's Burn.

I gently threw the jacket back into the room.

Who's has it? Mark wrote on the wall. Bright orange against the fresh yellow. Pap wouldn't be pleased.

Mark turned back into the room and walked over to the desk, kicking it for good measure. He stopped by our cupboard.

We held our breath and reached for each others' hands but it wasn't necessary. He didn't look inside. He reached for his jacket and he was gone.

Norva and I waited until the coast was absolutely clear before emerging from the cupboard. We stood against the wall of The Hub, by the doors.

'Who's has it?' I said. 'His grammar is atrocious.'

'It is! Remind me, what did Serena's letter say?' Norva asked.

I reached for my phone, 'Look'

Tick! Tock! Tick! Tock! Give Me The Flipping Clock. You're time runs out on Friday.

'It fits,' she said. 'So he did write it?'

'Confirmation,' I said.

I looked around. Hugo's desk was on its back in the middle of the room. One of its legs was broken. Snapped. The drawers lay next to it, emptied of its holdings.

'Honestly, I thought he would have been more thorough,' said Norva. 'Where's the smashed windows, the chairs tossed around the room? Why didn't he slash the seat, and look for The Clock in there?'

Hugo_down_2307.doc

Victim: Hugo Knightley-Webb
Body location: Corner One Refuse Area
Date and Time of discovery: 23/07 14:27

Time of death: Between Fri 20/07 22:30 23:05
and Sat 00:15 00:15 06:30

Weapon: Paint can - mostly likely. Suggested
by Katie: 24/07 09:02

Maybe not!

Motive: Money? Money for the clock? The Clock.
Hugo was coming into money

Incident! Hugo's van explodes Tue 24/07 21:32

Hypothesis: Flat 212 Murdered in Corner One
flat, either floor 21 or 22, with paint can,
placed in chute

~~To-do: Find out about the meeting~~
To-do: Find out where the suspects went after
the meeting
~~To-do: Ask Pap about his conversation and
limp~~
~~To-do: Test The Hugo/Chute hypothesis~~
~~To-do: Ask Pap about the paint/bags~~

306

To-do: ~~Close the time of death window~~

To-do: ~~Whitford Market~~

To-do: Find out what were Mark and Serena talking about 23/07 c15:11

To-do: Find out about the clock!

To-do: Find out who wrote Serena's note

To-do: Get Pap's phone

To-do: ~~Find out why Pap's bootprints were on Third Avenue~~

	221 ~~Pap~~ ~~Nik~~ ~~Norva~~ ~~Ringo~~	222 ~~Mrs Kowalski~~	223 Mark Walker ~~'Mother Walker'~~	211 ~~George Shah~~ ~~Nina Shah~~	212 ~~Hugo KW~~ **Serena KW**	213 ~~Charity~~ ~~Jane~~
Suspect's alibi during TOD window	Out until 01:27 'Getting rid of bad rubbish' 23:30 Friday. Pap apologized to Hugo via email. Was with Mrs K.	Working on a project with 'a friend'. Until 01:15. The friend is Pap.		GS: Backstage with TrojKat NS: With Aunt Geeta	In bed asleep. Heard something at 01:15.	Crying on her own, waiting for her friend – who was likely Pap.
Corroborated?	With Mrs K	~~No – but we suspect who her 'friend' is Pap.~~		Y – photographic evidence for both suspects.		
Motivation?	Argument at Friday's meeting over money.					Hugo owed her Money.
Questions?	Pap got the limp between Fri 22:30 and Sat 08:00, how? Were you painting Hugo's and Serena's flat on Saturday? YES		What were you talking to Serena about?		What were you talking to Mark about? Ants (dead and alive in your flat?) ~~Do you have a job?~~ Not really.	~~How did you get into our flat?~~ KEY ~~Does Hugo owe you money?~~ NOT REALLY ~~Why does Hugo owe you £250?~~ A PLEDGE ~~Why have you got Paps boots?~~ BORROWED ~~Did you make the prints on the avenue?~~ YES

308

55

The smell of fried food wafted through our door at seven.

I was awake, having barely slept. I kept an ear and an eye out for Pap.

And Mark.

Jane knocked on our door.

'Made you some breakfast,' she chirped cheerfully. 'I know you get up early.'

Norva rose vampire-like from her bed and rubbed her hands together, interest piqued.

'Yes, Jane! Incoming!' she called croakily. 'I'm thirst-ay,' she said with a hacking cough.

She looked at me and rubbed her hands together.

'Norva, now we've had a bit of sleep, let's go through things,' I said. 'We need to prioritise understanding The Clock. While you were sleeping,

I did some research; the world's most expensive clock went for 6.8 million dollars.'

'For real? That's nuts! Do you think this clock might be worth the same amount?'

'That's the thing, Norva. I'm not sure what we're looking for is even a clock.'

'What do you mean?' she said. 'Serena said it was a clock?'

'I know, but I just never heard Hugo talk much about clocks, ever. He liked architecture, paintings, fabric, vases…'

'Breakfast!' Jane trilled from the hallway.

'OK, let's feast and then figure it out,' said Norva.

'Alright,' I said. 'Fine.'

Norva climbed out of bed, opened the door and sprinted down the hallway.

Jane had put in work. On the table was the biggest breakfast spread I'd ever seen – in real life anyway.

The fullest breakfast:

• Eggs, fried

• Bacon

• Sausages

• Tomatoes, fried

• Beans

- Mushrooms
- Toast
- Vitonica, for me

I quickly snatched the bottle from the table.

'Hash browns, too!?' said Norva, as Jane placed another plate on the table.

- Hash browns

'This is nuts! Thank you!' Norva sat at the table and quickly filled her plate. And her mouth. 'You know when I said no 'step-mumming' Jane? This is fine. I didn't mean this. This is acceptable.'

Jane smiled. 'You're welcome!'

Ding! Ding!

Jane's phone. Her hand flew to her mouth.

'Oh no!' she gasped. 'The Hub's been vandalised!'

Quick glace at Norva.

'Oh no,' said Norva flatly, looking at Jane. 'That's too bad! Do you know who did it?' She craned her neck to look at her phone.

I stared at my plate.

'No, no details,' Jane said, pushing herself away from the table. 'I'm going to head down, see if I can go in.

Jane sighed as she put on her sandals. 'I worked so hard on that place.'

She bent down to stroke Ringo and left, closing the door behind her.

'Maybe we should have stopped him?' I said.

'Nah,' Norva replied. 'Collateral damage. Plus – you can't mess with timelines like that. If we did, who knows which dimension we'd exist in this morning.'

'I suppose.'

Norva reached for a sausage.

'This. Munch. Is. So. Good.' Norva banged the table between words. She held onto the table, but pushed her arms away. Her eyes rolled back in her head. 'So good,' she whispered.

'Is it?'

Norva reached for a hash brown. Grease dripped down her fingers.

'Recalibrate your taste buds, honestly,' she said.

I poked at a mushroom.

'I was surprised you're being decent to Jane this morning, Norva.'

'Why?'

I laughed. 'I still don't trust her 100%.'

'You don't?'

'Nope. Just yesterday she was standing around in our flat in the dark. Secretly using a key. Obstructing the course of justice with her prints.' I smiled at Norva. 'And all this food? What if she's poisoning us so she has Pap all to herself? What if she killed Hugo out of misguided solidarity with Pap?'

Norva dropped the hash brown. She stared into space. I'd caused her to malfunction.

'A joke, Norva.' I waved my hand in front of her face. No movement.

'It was just a joke,' I said quietly.

Ding! Ding!

Norva's phone broke the silence, and her trance.

'George,' she said. She read it out, in his voice: 'Girl, you smart!'

Norva looked at me, switching back to herself. 'I know this. I've met me.'

She reverted to George-mode: 'Leaving the recording on was a big move. You know, I can't send unlaid tracks. Bad luck. So come down. Now!'

Ding! Ding!

Another text. I leant over her shoulder to see.

ALSO – crazy movement next door this morning! Something doing!

Norva sent a text back.

Incoming! Clue please?

Ding! Ding!

Mark. Serena. The Clock.

I jumped to my feet. 'Let's go! It's unravelling, Norva – let's move.'

She sat still.

'Norva, what's wrong with you?'

I took a sip of my Vitonica.

'Nik, I think we've been looking at this the wrong way, I reckon –'

There was a knock at the door.

Ringo barked loudly.

56

I looked through the peephole.

Mark.

He fidgeted by the door, and banged again. I craned my body away from it.

I signalled to Norva. Her eyes widened. My heart raced.

Norva tiptoed up the hall and crouched behind me. Ringo barked and scratched at the door.

Mark banged again. I flinched.

'Why are you hiding?' I whispered.

'He can't see me like this,' she mouthed.

'Hello!' he shouted. 'I can hear you! Let me in! I know you're in there!'

I put the chain on the door and opened it slightly with trembling hands.

'You lied to me!' He hissed. 'I need to talk to you about The Clock. It wasn't there…'

'Oh, it wasn't?' I said. 'So sorry!'

I began to close the door. He pushed it open with his palm.

'Listen,' he said softly. 'I need some help. When's your dad getting back? Do you know?'

Norva stood by the door barely breathing, listening hard.

'We don't know. He's still in custody.'

Because of you.

Mark cursed under his breath.

'I need to get back to work – with your Dad. I'm broke. Did he leave any jobs for me? Has he said anything?' He looked anxious.

The audacity.

'Mark, we haven't thought about you at all, to be honest.'

Lies.

Behind me, Norva kicked my leg. I leaned away from Mark to look at her. She made a pleading face. She made a heart sign with her thumbs and first fingers.

I rapidly – but thoroughly – questioned her sanity.

'Can I come in for a second, please?'

He couldn't see my face. I was looking at Norva. She mouthed 'yes' and nodded her head, then ducked into our bedroom. I could hear, and smell, her spraying copious amounts of deodorant.

I opened the door.

Mark stepped in and sniffed the air. 'Super fresh in here,' he said. He strode into the living room. Ringo jumped at his legs, begging to be petted but Mark ignored him. He threw his phone on the coffee table, and flopped down into the sofa, his knees far apart.

I stood in the doorway. Norva stood beside me, smelling like pomegranate. She nodded at Mark. He nodded back.

'Yeah, like, I'm sorry 'bout your dad. Know that. But I'm in big trouble here, without him. No joke, I'm screwed.' He looked defeated.

'Why? What have you done?' I asked.

He reeled off his reasons on his fingers. 'I'm broke, mum's struggling – she's getting worse, I need to stay out of trouble, and I'm failing at that.' He leaned forward and put his head in his hands. 'I'm rubbish without your Dad and I've gotta find The Clock. I don't even know why they want it.'

They?

'Who's 'they', Mark?' said Norva.

'The people after Serena!' he whispered. 'The ones who killed Hugo.'

What?

Norva stared at me. I looked at Mark.

'Someone's trying to kill Serena?' I asked.

And it isn't you? I thought to myself.

'Yeah!' he said. 'They left her a note and everything. It's really bad.'

I reached for my phone. 'Here,' I said. 'Call Katie – she's the police woman who used to live here, remember? She'll help you.'

'Nah, he said. It's too late for that.'

He looked crestfallen.

I felt a small pang of pity for him, but I shook it away. He's a criminal.

Mark looked up. 'Can I use your loo?'

Did he not literally just come from his house?

I sighed.

'If you must.' I pointed down the hall.

Ding! Ding!

Mark's phone beeped and vibrated on the table. A message from someone called 'SirIna.'

His spelling, honestly.

No. I can't do that, Mark.

Norva pointed to the phone. I reached for mine and took a photo.

The toilet flushed.

'You know what? While I was weeing...'

Too much information.

'...I thought about it. Me being here. It makes no sense. You can't help me. You're two little girls. Without your dad.'

Norva looked deflated.

Mark reached for his phone on the table.

He noticed the message. His face was stern. 'I better go. I have to finish some business. When you speak to him next though, tell him I said keep his head up.'

Mark walked to the door. 'Joe's innocent,' he said.

'We know,' Norva said quietly.

I shut the door.

'Norva, did you hear that? Mark said...' I began.

Ding! Ding!

Norva's phone. A message from George.

ERM DO YOU WANT TO KNOW OR NOT? COME DOWN!

57

Norva gently knocked on George's front door.

Unsurprisingly, he didn't answer. I kicked my foot against his Welcome Bach doormat, while Norva jabbed out a message on to him on her phone.

Goerge appeared instantly.

'Why you texting? Just knock properly innit!' he said loudly.

Norva shushed him, put her finger to her lips, and pushed him into the hallway. She stepped into his bedroom.

'What do you have for us?' she whispered, millimeters from his face. She pointed to the wall joining his room to Serena's flat.

George laughed, but kept his voice low. 'Always serving drama. Never not. Sit yourself down and prick your ears up.'

He placed a pair of headphones on her head, and started his recording. Norva sat with her elbows on the desk, thumbs under her chin, index fingers drumming her lips. She closed her eyes and shook her head at what she heard.

Norva removed the headphones and sat silently for a moment. She spun around in his chair.

'Just as I thought,' she said.

'My turn.' I pushed her off the chair and sat at the desk. George scrubbed backwards through the file.

'And go!' he said.

I put the headphones on. The conversation, verbatim. Word for word.

```
Mark: 'Thanks for the medicine, Serena, but
you're in over your head. You know that,
don't you? This ain't gonna end well. For
you.'

Serena: 'I need that part - urgently...'
Serena laughs or cries at this point, uncon-
firmed. 'That's the problem. You shouldn't
have done what you did.'

Mark: 'But I have no idea what this Clock
```

thing is? It doesn't even look like a clock
to me. I know nothing about your fancy
world. This is too much. I want out.'

Serena: 'So do I. But it's too late. We're
both in deep.'

I took the headphones off and looked over
at Norva. She leaned against the wall with her arms
crossed.

'Bring up the receipts, Nik. Show me Mark's pills
from yesterday,' asked Norva.

'Mark's on drugs!?' George exclaimed, hand to
his mouth. 'This just gets worse!' he whispered.

I zoomed into the photograph and showed
it to Norva. 'OK, Niacin, Niacin, Niacin,' she said.
'Remember that please.'

'I need your computer and a glass of water – my
throat's like the Sahara.'

He laughed and nodded.

Norva Googled Niacin. 'It's just B3 vitamin,' she
said. 'No one's dying from vitamins.'

'Does it have any side effects, though?' I asked.

Norva reeled them off. 'Itching, fast heart, gut
pains, the runs, the pukes. Gout.'

'Gout?' I asked

'Yeah, it's kind of a rich man's disease,' said Norva, shooting me a sarcastic smile. 'Fits Hugo, but it's not fatal.'

She continued, 'Proper skin flushing, plus the spins.'

'Flushed red skin and dizziness?' I said. 'Oh no, Norva. Remember how pink Hugo looked in George's video?'

'A proper salmon,' said Norva, nodding.

George returned with water for Norva and a Vitonica for me. 'Mum picked one up for you, remember to thank her innit!'

'Sure will,' I said.

'George, pull up your video of Hugo at the meeting,' demanded Norva.

'I'll do you one better!' he said. 'I gifed it for you.' George pulled out his phone.

Hugo is red and unstable on his feet. He sits down. Serena rubs his back. She gives him a juice. The gif starts again. Hugo is red and unstable once more.

'Classy George,' I said.

He shrugged. 'Whatever, Nik. It's helping you, no? Pipe down.'

'Do you think Mark poisoned Hugo with Niacin, Norva?' I asked. 'And Serena is next?'

'Doubt it,' Norva said. 'You'd need tonnes of it.'

She turned her back to us and faced George's computer. 'I'm going to search Hugo's symptoms. Skin flushing, unsteady, coughing. I wish we flipping did this before!' she shouted, looking at me.

She typed away. I looked over at George, who was still enjoying his gif.

Norva gasped. Her hand flew to her mouth.

'Cyanide!' she whispered.

58

'The hell you know about cyanide!?' George said, stepping away from Norva.

Norva spun around to look at me. 'Nik, remember that night Katie burned the popcorn, and the flat stunk for like a week?'

I nodded, though it was no more than three hours.

'We watched that old film, the one where that guy's wife got poisoned at that fancy dinner. "Sparkling Cyanide", remember it?'

I nodded. I remembered the scorched snacks more than the film, honestly.

George broke in, 'Yo, cool story, big theory – but you can't get cyanide off Amazon. That's pure Agatha Christie business.'

I agreed. 'It's not the 1920s, Norva. Cyanide is not an off-the-shelf item.'

'Obviously,' she said sarcastically. 'But hear me out. Tell me if this is not what we're dealing with.'

She paraphrased from the website: 'At low doses, before you pass out, you'll get weakness, headaches, confusion. You'll be giddy. It gets hard to breathe. Blah blah blah you start dying slowly, from a heart attack. You have cherry red skin. Cherry. Red. Skin,' she said, banging on the desk, between words.

'Easy,' said George, steadying his microphone.

'But where do you get cyanide from? Search for sources,' I said.

She turned back to the computer.

I laughed. 'If anyone sees your searches, you're going to prison, Norva.'

I took a sip of my Vitonica.

'Why do you think I'm using this one's computer?' She jerked her thumb at George.

'Oi!' he shouted.

We shushed him in unison.

'Nik,' she said quietly. 'Sources of cyanide. Can be natural or made by humans. Naturally, it's produced by some bacteria, algae, fungi. It's also found in a number of food and plants, particularly the seeds of fruit, such as peaches and cherries.'

I grabbed George's phone and looked at his gif. Hugo is still red and unstable on his feet. He still sits down. Serena still rubs his back.

She gives him a juice.

She gives him a juice.

Peaches and cherries.

Cherries and peaches.

She gives him a juice.

I dropped my bottle of Vitonica.

59

'Forget Hugo. Mum's going to end you for spilling that juice on my carpet,' George snapped, running to get a cloth.

It didn't matter. Norva and I stared at each other silently.

I spoke first. My mouth was dry.

'Serena with the Vitonica. Not Mark? Not Mark at all. This whole time?' My throat started to close. 'Am I going to die, Norva?' I panicked and started to cry. 'I drank so much.'

My stomach burned and my head pounded.

Norva shook her head. 'No, you'll be alright. You have to take a high dosage at one time. And it works quickly.'

'I can't believe we discounted her so many times, Norva. Fratricide? On The Tri? How could she do this to Hugo?'

She put her hand on my back.

'What's next? What do we do?' I asked.

Norva smiled, rubbing my shoulder. 'This is it Nik. This is it!' she said excitedly. 'We've actually cracked it. I've – sorry – *we've* dreamed of this moment. Do you still have the confrontation checklist? Remember how we'd never thought we'd need that!'

Norva clapped her hands together with glee.

'I think so. It's probably out of date now.' I searched through the files on my phone. I found it.

'OK, Norva.'

Confrontation_checklist_v1.doc

Step one. Send a message to your loved ones.

Norva set up a group message.

Pap, Katie, Her, Me.

'Put Jane in there,' I said.

'Eurgh, fine!'

She read the words as she thumbed them out.

'Everyone. We know who killed Hugo. Not you

Pap, obvs – where are you? Katie, we sent you evidence, yesterday. It was Serena with the juices for money from The Clock.'

'Next?' she demanded.

Step two. Get your story straight.

'Crystal clear. The sister, with the juices, in the flat. She poisoned him after the meeting. Wrapped him up and threw him in the chute at twelve fifteen on Friday. She's strong enough to do it. Next?'

Step three. Be clear on the motive.

'Money. Cold hard cash,' she said. 'OK. What's the next step?'

'That's the whole list, Norva.'

'Oh for real?' she said, disappointment in her voice. 'We need to work on that. Make notes on the process today, yes.'

Norva's phone vibrated. Incoming call.

'Katie,' she said cancelling it. 'Not now.'

Ding! Ding!

A message from Katie.

Do not do ANYTHING. Stay where you are. We're coming.

'Yeah, right Katie! Who's coming with me?' Norva said, standing.

'I'm coming.' I jumped off the bed.

We looked at George. He knelt on the floor wiping at the spilled Vitonica. He pointed to his microphone and reached for his headphones.

'I'll get the confession from here – gotta think of the track!' he said, tapping his temple.

60

Norva banged on Serena's door.

'Listen,' she whispered. 'This is the play. I'm gonna throw Mark under the bus. Frame him. Let's see if we understand how he's involved in this hot mess. Go with it!'

'Norva…' My heart flipped over in my chest. 'I–'

'Hi, girls!' Serena trilled. 'You just caught me – we're just packing up the last of my stuff – after the van last night, The Hub this morning it's time to–'

'We just caught you alright,' Norva said, steely, cutting her off. 'Can we come in?'

'Sure,' Serena said. 'You can give us a hand! The more the merrier.'

The flat was empty, mostly. All of Hugo's possessions had been packed away.

The antiques, the magazines, the awkward small sofa. Gone.

Mark was in the living room. He nodded at us as he glumly packed up a box.

'Did you find it?' I whispered.

He shook his head and looked up at Serena, who stood behind us. She was desperately trying to communicate with Mark through her eyes. And failing.

'A drink, girls?' Serena asked. She looked at me and sung, 'I have a final batch of Vitonicas?'

'Not on your life,' said Norva, answering for me.

Norva turned to Mark.

'Serena, I think you need to be careful of being alone with Mark,' she said.

His eyes grew wide. He started to back away.

'This again, girls?' Serena said, staring at me.

'What? What you mean again? Why you saying that for?' he shouted.

'We have reason to believe he's involved in Hugo's murder,' Norva said.

'What!?' He screamed. 'Why? What makes you say that?'

'Your threatening letter – and this graffiti in The Hub. Show her, Nik.'

I showed her the photo on the phone. 'The grammatical errors are the same,' I said.

'Mark!' she said, stepping towards us, away from him. 'You didn't do this, did you? You wouldn't?'

Norva and I looked at each other.

'Serena, what do you mean? You showed me the letter, that's why I'm helping! You made me rob The Hub last night! Tell them the truth!'

'Mark, I can't believe you would do this to me!' Serena broke down in convincing sobs. 'Girls, thank you! Thank you for piecing it together for me.' She looked at me. 'I should have listened to you, Nik.'

Serena turned to Mark.

'How could you do this to me? I trusted you!' she shouted, spitting slightly. 'Norva, can you call your Police friend and arrest this, this murderer?'

'They're all on the way. They know the whole story,' said Norva.

'The whole story?' asked Serena calmly.

'Oh yeah, there's more, Serena,' said Norva.

'More?' she said.

'We know how Hugo died. Like, really died.' she said.

'You do?' asked Serena. 'What happened?'

'Poison,' Norva replied flatly.

Serena gripped the kitchen counter.

'Poison?' she whispered, clutching her chest. 'How do you know that?'

'Timings,' said Norva. 'They don't add up.'

Serena was translucent. White. Like she'd just seen Hugo's ghost.

'Wait, what?' Mark shouted. 'Hugo died by the paint can, didn't he?'

Norva shook her head and turned to Mark. Serena stared at Norva.

'You know he didn't, Mark. Don't you? Why did you poison Hugo? With Niacin?'

'Niacin!' Serena shrieked. 'No, Mark no! Not Niacin. You didn't? Tell me they're lying, Mark. Tell me!' she screamed, clearly angling for a Best Actress nomination at the BAFTAs.

Norva rolled her eyes.

'Hold on! How do you know I take Niacin?' asked Mark, his hand in the air. 'I've never told anyone about that.'

'We found it in your pocket. Last night,' said Norva. 'When you took it off in The Hub, silly.'

'What? You were there last night in The Hub?' asked a surprised Serena.

We nodded.

'Yep, we saw it all,' I said.

'I take it for spots, OK?' Mark said. 'Happy now?'

'But you don't have spots…?' said Norva, staring at his face. 'Your skin is beautiful,' she sighed.

'Yeah because I take those meds, innit! Serena clued me into them.' He pointed at her.

'Don't bring her into this, Mark!' Norva demanded. 'We're on to you! We know you did it!'

I nodded. 'Mark, you're going to prison for a long time,' I said. 'At least fifteen years.'

'No! I didn't kill anyone! All I did was The Hub…and the van.' He pointed at Serena. 'To save her life!'

'Because you guys are in love or something?' asked Norva nervously.

'In *LOVE?*' Mark shouted. 'She's old enough to be my mum. No, gross.'

Norva looked relieved and pleased.

'Look, flip this,' he shouted. 'I'm coming clean. I'm not spending fifteen years in prison for nothing – well, not 'nothing.' I did a bad thing.' Mark looked at his hands, and then at me.

'I was helping your Dad on Saturday. She,' he pointed at Serena, 'was all over him, trying to give him a massage for his mashed-up leg in the other room. I saw this beautiful brooch. I knew my mum would love it. It was well up her street.'

He hung his head.

'It's her birthday soon, and she's been stuck in our flat since her accident, so basically forever. So, I grabbed it and stuffed it in my pocket. I didn't know Serena was behind me. I tried to give it back, but she said I could keep it. She wouldn't tell your Dad – or the cops – if, if I helped her find something...'

'The Clock,' I said.

'Yeah. She showed me the note. That's why I did the Hub over. I still don't get why I had to set fire to the van.'

'Lies, Mark!' Serena cried. 'There was no brooch – that never happened.'

'But it's true!'

'Describe the brooch to us, Mark,' I said.

'Why?' Serena shouted. 'It doesn't exist! Hugo didn't do brooches,' she spat.

'It's the shape of a star, with diamonds on the outside.'

I held my phone up to the group, displaying the photo from last night. 'This one?' I asked.

'Yeah, that's it!' Mark shouted. 'That's the one!'

'Thanks, Mark. That's all we need to know. Sorry to spook you,' said Norva. She put her hand on his shoulder. 'Collateral damage, you understand.'

He shook his head.

We turned to look at Serena. Her face fell.

'Got you, Serena,' Norva said. 'You're a terrible liar – and actress.' She looked her up and down. 'And you bring shame to your name. The greatest tennis player of all time would never!'

Serena was silent.

The front door burst open behind us.

61

Katie, DCI Sharp and Officer Burnett ran into the room. They were finally acting on our message.

Katie shouted at us, 'What did I say to you, both. What did I say!? I told–'

A tall black man pushed through the group and stood next her.

Pap! He was free. At last.

'Pap!' we screamed.

'ALEXANDERS ASSEMBLE!' he screamed back at us.

'You're back! You're here? You're free!?' Norva shouted through tears.

Pap swept us into a group hug.

Jane wept behind him. 'This is beautiful,' she said, dabbing at her eyes.

Norva wiped tears away. She shook her braids. 'OK, OK, where were we? Let me wrap this up real quick.'

Now she felt safe – and had an audience – she was in her element.

'For the benefit of our new arrivals, I'll go from the top,' said Norva, looking at DCI Sharp. 'Hugo never died by blunt force from a paint can. That was a fortunate coincidence, wasn't it, Serena? A perfect decoy.'

Serena was silent.

Mark stood next to her. His mouth hung open at the unfolding scene.

'You killed him using Vitonica, didn't you? Well, from its waste. The seeds, kernels and pits you extracted during production. And then you fed it to him. Your own brother. Beautiful work, Serena,' said Norva, sarcastically applauding her. 'Really. Well done. Getting everyone on The Tri on your side through the juice – and the dog walking and the yoga classes. Perfect. Smart.'

Serena was silent.

Mark could not believe it.

'Serena?' he whispered. 'You never? The threats were a lie? I'm involved in this for no reason?'

Serena was silent.

I spoke up. 'That's what the Tupperware container of pulp was. And why you had so many blenders in the van. The seeds kept breaking them.'

Norva nodded. 'So you got the village idiot here to torch it, to hide the evidence. Lovely.'

Mark shook his head in disbelief. 'Maybe I am an idiot,' he whispered.

'There were no threats. You wrote that letter yourself – using terrible grammar on purpose to keep him in the frame, right, Serena?

'Note...?' Asked DCI Sharp.

'She never showed you the note?' I asked, and then I understood. 'Ah – *that's* why she kept it, and it was never filed as evidence. We just assumed you were stretched and forgot.'

'I don't forget evidence,' she replied, her left eye twitching slightly.

'Oh my God!' shouted Mark.

Serena was silent.

A murmur ran through the room.

'Pap and Mark cleaned the scene for you, as planned by Hugo. You and your fruits brought the ants up here and your cyanide killed them. Hugo didn't know that he would be covering up his own murder when he ordered his repairs, months ago, did he, Serena?'

Serena was silent.

Norva looked at the crowd, but mostly at DCI Sharp.

'It's almost perfect. Almost. Except, you couldn't find what you were looking for, could you? The Clock?'

Serena laughed.

'Almost perfect, girls,' she clapped. 'You're right. Almost perfect.'

'Why would you do this to your brother?' said Jane. 'For a timepiece? That's just ridiculous.'

'You're all so naive. So simple,' she looked Jane up and down. 'That's why I love it here,' she laughed. 'No, no. The Clock is not a timepiece. It's not a watch of any kind. It's a vase by Alys Clockenstein – hence the colloquial name,' Serena said. 'It's a seminal and unique piece by her. Hugo's pride and joy. Her only vase with a lid. Priceless. Well, no, not *priceless*,' she chuckled. 'But worth half a million or so.' Her eyes shone. 'A life-changing amount.'

So she changed Hugo's life to have it.

'I found the bottom, but I can't find the lid. Without it, well, it might as well be worthless.'

She chuckled.

A vase with a lid.

A chill ran through my body, but something burned a hole in my pocket.

I looked over at Norva. She looked back at me, confused at my reaction.

I felt faint and stumbled on the spot. I reached into my pocket.

I turned the lid over in my hand. I looked at it closely for the first time.

1/1 Clockenstein was inscribed on the inside.

I thrust my palm at Serena.

'You mean this?'

Serena was whiter than skimmed milk. Her eyes two burning black holes in her face; she launched herself at me. Like the wild, rabid animal she truly was.

'You had it the whole time?' She screamed. 'The whole time!'

Pap jumped between us quickly, followed by DCI Sharp and her colleagues.

'Book her boys!' shouted Norva above the fray. 'Katie! Miranda her up!'

Katie looked at DCI Sharp who nodded.

Katie stepped forward. She beamed and stood up straight.

'Serena Jocasta Knightley-Webb, you do not have to say anything. But it may harm your defence if, you do not mention when questioned something which you later rely on in court. Anything you do say may be given in evidence.'

Katie slipped the handcuffs on Serena's wrist.

'Impressive work,' said DCI Sharp to Norva. Her voice was cool, but there was warmth in her eyes.

Norva squealed with delight. 'I try,' she said, bowing.

Katie led Serena to the door and onto the Avenue. The crowd that had gathered below booed to the sound of a hundred camera phone flashes. Hugo's flat began to empty. Jane turned to Pap. 'I told you about her, didn't I? Didn't I?' She said, swatting him. She gave him a huge cuddle. 'I missed you,' she said, into his neck.

'Get a room,' said Norva, sticking her tongue out.

DAILY NEWS CHRONICLE

NO. 57,896

BEST SELING NEWSPAPER ON THE BLOCK

TODAY'S NEWS

HIGH–RISE MYSTERY SOLVED

Murderer Found

Serena Knightley-Webb resident of the Triangle Estate has been charged with the murder of fellow resident and brother Hugo Knightley-Webb

Funding Increase

The Triangle Estate is to receive £800,000 extra funding from council following investigations into standards following Hugo Knightley-Webb murder.

Vandal Charges

Mark Walker convicted with vandalism. Gets a tag and suspended sentence.

62

We stood in the rain, at the back of the crowd.
Droplets ran down the back of my neck, under my shirt.
I shivered in delight.

Norva was less pleased. She looked at me,
annoyed, underneath her mangled umbrella. As she
spun around to talk to me, a free rib threatened to take
my eye. I ducked.

'Honestly, can't believe you like this wet mess.
What's wrong with you?' she grumped.

'What?' I laughed. 'It's refreshing!'

Norva looked to the sky. 'Weather Gods!' she
bellowed. 'It's mid-August! I'm so sorry I cussed. I regret
it, OK? I take it back. Campaign starts now to bring
back the sun. How many signatures do you need? I'll do
it!'

'It will be sunny next week, don't worry,' I offered. 'I checked the forecast.'

'Yeah, what good's that going to be? We'll be stuck in school!'

I shrugged.

Sissy wheeled by, talking to Barry.

'You two should be at the front,' she said with a smile, pushing us forward with her hand. 'This is all thanks to you.'

'Next time, get me some money for Bermuda's will you?' shouted Barry. 'I need me a refurb.'

'There won't be a next time Barry,' I said. 'Hopefully.'

Barry nodded.

Norva watched them move away. 'They're right, you know. Let's move. I said I'd livestream George's debut,' said Norva.

George stood on the makeshift stage outside the room formerly known as The Hub.

'This one's called *Justice Jam*,' he shouted over his microphone. 'Featuring the one and only TrojKat!'

Justice Jam was his new song with his hero. It was words and phrases from Serena's confession, interspersed with TrojKat saying 'justice' in a multitude of ways.

'Hands in the air, Tri-gang!' he demanded excitedly.

Everyone's arms remained by their sides. Apart from Norva's.

'This one is a certified bop! What's wrong with you lot?' she shouted, jumping up and down with her umbrella and phone, singing along.

'Half a million or so. Justice. Vase with a Lid. Justice. Brooch? Brooch? Brooch? Justice'

I defended my eyes from the weapon she wielded.

George spotted us and pointed. 'N-squared in the house!'

Pap and Jane held hands next to the statue of Ellis Silvertöe. Katie stood next to them. She rolled her eyes and laughed.

The song ended. Finally.

'Peace out Tri, you've been great! Peep my Sound Cloud, yeah?' shouted George, as Pap pulled him off stage.

The Tri offered a smattering of applause. Mostly for Pap ending the noise.

Jane held the microphone. 'Hello, everyone! Thanks George, and thank you all so much for coming out – in this weather –' she laughed and looked at the sky ' – to the opening of The HKW Centre for The Arts.'

The crowd cheered.

'This new facility replaces The Hub, and the previously-empty adjacent units. Just so many thanks to give. Wow, where to start? To everyone that contributed to the Tri-Angels efforts to make this happen! Thank you to Joe, Mark and the volunteers for pulling the building work together!'

The crowd roared.

'Thanks to the Art Club for their wonderful collage. Thank you to Mrs Kowalski for the refreshments throughout.'

'The pierogis are particularly fresh today,' said Norva. 'She did good.'

'But most of all, I'd like to thank Norva and Anika Alexander.'

Heads turned to look at us.

Oh no. I hate attention.

'Today would just not be possible without them, their dogged determination and their considerable bravery.'

Jane's eyes filled with tears. 'I'm so proud of them, and I know Hugo would be too!'

The crowd applauded wildly.

Pap especially. He winked at us and beamed proudly.

'Come on up, Nik and Norva. Open The HKW. It's all on you.'

Norva grabbed my hand. 'Time to shine,' she said, throwing her braids over her shoulders. 'This is our moment!'

'Alexanders assemble,' I replied with a smile.

Hugo_down_2307_FINAL.doc
SOLVED!
Victim: Hugo Knightley-Webb
Culprit: Serena Knightley-Webb
Body location: Corner One Refuse Area

Date and Time of discovery: 23/07 14:27

Time of death: Between Fri 20/07 ~~22:30~~ 23:05
and Sat 00:15 ~~00:15~~ ~~06:30~~

Weapon: ~~Paint can - mostly likely. Suggested~~
~~by Katie: 24/07 09:02 Maybe not!~~ Cyanide,
created through seeds.

Motive: ~~Money? Money for the clock?~~ The Clock.
Hugo was coming into money

Incident! Hugo's van explodes Tue 24/07 21:32
Hypothesis: Flat 212 ~~Murdered in Corner One~~
~~flat~~, ~~either floor 21 or 22~~, ~~with paint can~~,
placed in chute << CORRECT

~~To-do: Find out about the meeting~~
To-do: Find out where the suspects went after
the meeting
~~To-do: Ask Pap about his conversation and~~
~~limp~~
~~To-do: Test The Hugo/Chute hypothesis~~
~~To-do: Ask Pap about the paint/bags~~

351

~~To-do: Close the time of death window~~
~~To-do: Whitford Market~~
~~To-do: Find out what were Mark and Serena talking about 23/07 c15:11~~
~~To-do: Find out about the clock!~~
~~To-do: Find out who wrote Serena's note~~
To-do: Get Pap's phone
~~To-do: Find out why Pap's bootprints were on Third Avenue~~

	221 ~~Pap~~ ~~Nik~~ ~~Norva~~ ~~Ringo~~	222 ~~Mrs Kowalski~~	223 ~~Mark Walker~~ ~~'Mother Walker'~~	211 ~~George Shah~~ ~~Nina Shah~~	212 ~~Hugo KW~~ **Serena KW**	213 ~~Charity Jane~~
Suspect's alibi during TOD window	Out until 01:27 'Getting rid of bad rubbish' 23:30 Friday. Pap apologized to Hugo via email. Was with Mrs K.	Working on a project with 'a friend'. Until 01:15. The friend is Pap.		GS: Backstage with TrojKat NS: With Aunt Geeta	In bed asleep. Heard something at 01:15. LIAR!	Crying on her own, waiting for her friend – who was likely Pap.
Corroborated?	With Mrs K	~~No – but we suspect who her 'friend' is Pap.~~		Y – photographic evidence for both suspects.		
Motivation?	Argument at Friday's meeting over money.					Hugo owed her Money.
Questions?	Pap got the limp between Fri 22:30 and Sat 08:00, how? Were you painting Hugo's and Serena's flat on Saturday? YES		What were you talking to Serena about?		What were you talking to Mark about? Ants (dead and alive in your flat?) ~~Do you have a job?~~ Not really.	~~How did you get into our flat?~~ KEY ~~Does Hugo owe you money?~~ NOT REALLY ~~Why does Hugo owe you £250?~~ A PLEDGE ~~Why have you got Paps boots?~~ BORROWED ~~Did you make the prints on the avenue?~~ YES

353

NIK AND NORVA

WILL BE BACK

ACKNOWLEDGEMENTS

As tempting as it is to thank myself, the complete truth is you would not be reading this acknowledgement page, in this here book, if it wasn't for the following thoroughly excellent people.

Aimée Felone and **David Stevens**– it's an absolute honor to be part of the Knights Of family. Thank you for caring, your campaigning and the opportunity to share Nik and Norva with the world. #readtheonepercent

Hellie Ogden – I cannot thank you and your team at Janklow & Nesbit enough. You are a complete boss.

Robin Stevens – your What if X was Y? questions constantly changed the game, for the better. **Rachel Mann** – your comments were invaluable. Thank you!

Special thanks to **Marssaié Jordan** and **Wumi Olaosebikan** not only for their excellent creative direction and design, but also not killing me over fonts.

Daniel Anthony – thank you for the space, support and infinite tea.

Joseph Jackson Anthony – thank you for your ideas, your Post It notes and your frighteningly-comprehensive list of potential murder methods. Should I be worried?

Margot Jackson Anthony – woof.

Lynda Hunter – thank you for your early reading, your ear, your lemon loaf.

Lynsey Smyth and **Kate Booth** are my favourite people, and I cannot thank you enough for the friendship, the gifs, the gin, the support. I miss you.

Shout out to **Steve Webb** who only understands about 70% of what I say. Thank you for patiently sketching out The Tri and explaining what risers are.

Julian Jackson, **Dean Jackson** and **Leigh Jackson** remain the best.

Thank you and sorry to everyone at **Site Gallery** for the times I came to work, zombie-like after an all-night write.

Anna Maria – you're the shippiest ship that ever shipped.

And finally, **Pamella Jackson**. I think you would have loved this.

SHARNA JACKSON

Sharna Jackson is an author and Artistic Director who specialises in developing and delivering socially-engaged digital initiatives for children and young people across culture, publishing and entertainment.

She is driven specifically to encourage and increase diverse and disengaged audiences' participation in the arts locally, nationally, and globally.

Sharna has written three books, *Tate Kids British Art Activity Book*, *Tate Kids Modern Art Activity Book* and *High Rise Mystery* - the first in a middle-grade series featuring a sibling detective duo everyone's dying to meet.

She is the Artistic Director at Site Gallery, Sheffield's leading international contemporary art space, specialising in moving image, new media and performance.

She is on the board of Sheffield Doc/Fest, Upswing Aerial Arts and New Writing North in addition to being a member of BAFTA's Children's and Learning and New Talent committees and the Children's Media Conference advisory board.

Sharna was born and raised in Luton and currently lives in Sheffield and Rotterdam.

CAN'T WAIT FOR THE NEXT

HIGH-RISE MYSTERY?

CHECK OUT OTHER BOOKS FROM **KNIGHTS OF**:

KNIGHTS AND BIKES
by Gabrielle Kent

GHOST
by JASON REYNOLDS

AVAILABLE IN BOOKSHOPS NOW